THE INFINITY year OF AVALON James

THE INFINITY year OF AVALON James

DANA MIDDLETON

 FEIWEL AND FRIENDS · NEW YORK

A Feiwel and Friends Book
An Imprint of Macmillan

Our books may be purchased in bulk for promotional, educational, or business use. Please contact your local bookseller or the Macmillan Corporate and Premium Sales Department at (800) 221-7945 ext. 5442 or by e-mail at MacmillanSpecialMarkets@macmillan.com.

Library of Congress Cataloging-in-Publication Data
Names: Middleton, Dana, author.
Title: The infinity year of Avalon James / Dana Middleton.
Description: First edition. | New York : Feiwel and Friends, [2016] | Summary: Facing bullying at home and her family being torn apart, Avalon anxiously waits with her best friend, Atticus, for the magical power they are supposed to inherit between their tenth and eleventh birthdays.
Identifiers: LCCN 2015042044 (print) | LCCN 2016020750 (ebook) | ISBN 9781250085696 (hardback) | ISBN 9781250085689 (ebook)
Subjects: | CYAC: Best friends—Fiction. | Friendship—Fiction. | Bullying—Fiction. | Family problems—Fiction. | Magic—Fiction. | Secrets—Fiction. | BISAC: JUVENILE FICTION / Fantasy & Magic. | JUVENILE FICTION / Family / Parents. | JUVENILE FICTION / Social Issues / Bullying. | JUVENILE FICTION / Social Issues / Friendship.
Classification: LCC PZ7.1.M517 Inf 2016 (print) | LCC PZ7.1.M517 (ebook) | DDC [Fic]—dc23
LC record available at https://lccn.loc.gov/2015042044

Book design by Liz Dresner

Feiwel and Friends logo designed by Filomena Tuosto

First Edition—2016

10 9 8 7 6 5 4 3 2 1

mackids.com

For Mom and Papa

ONE

My name is Avalon James and this is my Infinity Year. The Infinity Year is such a secret thing that hardly anybody knows about it. But this is how it works. When you turn ten years old (like I did on May 29), you start your Infinity Year. I looked up *Infinity Year* in the dictionary and found nothing. I did find the definition for the word *Infinity*, though. It means "endless" or "forever."

There's one main rule to the Infinity Year. You can only talk about it with your best friend. Luckily, my best friend, Atticus, is ten years old, too. If we keep to this rule, and only talk about it with each other and nobody else, we will each develop a magical power before the year is out. It's called our Infinity Year power and it will disappear forever on the day we turn eleven. That means I will have my magical power for fourteen days longer than Atticus because he is fourteen days older than me.

It's been almost three months since my tenth birthday and I haven't gotten my Infinity power yet. I haven't levitated off the ground or turned Elena Maxwell into a bullfrog. I even tried to trade places with my cat, Marmalade (M for short), like in some kind of weird animal-girl body switch movie. So far, I'm still a girl but I am a little afraid of waking up in the body of a mighty fur-ball-hacking cat. Writing with paws could prove difficult.

Neither Atticus nor I had ever heard of the Infinity Year until last spring. Atticus believed in it right away. Of course he did. That's how he is. He has no lie detector whatsoever. It's not like he's dumb or anything. Atticus is supremely smart—about most things. Like books and *Titanic* trivia. He just sees the best in everybody. Even when he shouldn't.

I, on the other hand, am the kind of person who generally likes to see something first before I believe it. Just because someone says something doesn't mean it's true. And at first I wasn't sure I believed in this Infinity Year business. But it came from a very reliable source—from the most trustworthy person I have ever known. So I'm inclined to believe there must be some truth to it. And I like the idea of having a magical power.

I also like the idea of not being nine anymore. Being nine

years old was extremely unlucky for me. I wish I could have skipped that year altogether. Atticus said it was the year I had to grow up too fast.

He was right.

Over the past summer, as our Infinity Year started, things began to feel more normal again. I had left being nine years old behind and was starting to get used to the way things were at ten. My cat, M, was there for me. So was Atticus. Mom was working long hours at the hospital but she was trying. She really was. And I was starting to feel better.

Then we went to our school open house.

In our school—that would be Grover Cleveland K–8— all the parents and kids go to the school open house the week before school starts. Mr. Peterson, our principal, talks to everyone from the stage of the Grover Cleveland Lunchroom and Auditorium and tells us everything we are supposed to know about the year to come.

This year we were starting fifth grade. As usual, Atticus and I sat next to each other in the assembly and didn't really listen to Mr. Peterson. Atticus was drawing an infinity sign above my knee when his mother, Mrs. Brightwell, pulled the pen out of his hand. On nights like these, Mrs. Brightwell and my mother never sat next to each other. Atticus and I always sat between them. My father used to say that, in the jigsaw puzzle of life, Mrs. Brightwell and my mom were pieces that just didn't fit.

I have gone to this school my whole life. In fact, I am somewhat famous here for three main reasons.

First, M won third prize at our school animal talent show. She excels in coughing up the biggest fur balls in known cat history. The *Arcadia Weekly Herald* put a picture of M, her fur balls, and me right on the back page.

Second, I took a particular photo of Elena Maxwell and posted it on the fourth-grade bulletin board last year. Elena, who is always dressed better than anybody else, somehow wore white pants with American flag underwear underneath them. How did I know? When she was leaning over her art project, American flag held high, everyone knew. It was just my idea to take a picture of it. Because a picture lasts forever. I named the photo *Elena Maxwell: True American* and gave myself a photo credit just like they do in the big magazines. Unfortunately, Mrs. Bennett wasn't amused and removed it immediately. I don't know why. It's a well-known fact that Elena Maxwell is my nemesis and that I am hers. We are nemeses. It is also a well-known fact that she has done far worse to me.

Lastly . . .

Well, there *is* a third reason that people know about me but I don't want to talk about that one yet. It's what made being nine so bad.

The open house assembly lasted forever. If I hadn't had to pee so bad, I would have died of boredom. By the time Mr. Peterson introduced the last teacher, Ms. Zeldin, I was sure I was going to burst. Ms. Zeldin ran the sixth-grade science fair, which must have been the greatest darn science fair in human history the way Mr. Peterson went on and on about it. But I couldn't think about that right now.

When he finally finished, I looked at my mom and said, "I gotta go!"

"Okay. I'll be in here," she said as yelling kids of all sizes rushed past. The parents and teachers usually stayed in the auditorium and had refreshments while the kids ran down the halls to see what classrooms and teachers they would have for the year.

"I'll meet you there," I said to Atticus before I sprinted toward the bathroom. He knew what I meant. We'd meet outside of Ms. Smith's room down the fifth-grade hallway.

Ms. Smith has short red hair and round glasses with black rims. She has a fish named Alexander in an aquarium in her classroom and pictures of active volcanoes from around the world on her back wall. Last year, we would always hear laughter coming from Ms. Smith's class. Ms. Smith is the fifth-grade teacher everyone wants to get.

Since second grade, Atticus and I have always been in the same class. Somehow it just worked out that way. We wanted Ms. Smith's class—that was for sure—but as long as we were together, that's what really mattered.

After pushing through what seemed like every kid in the whole school, I slipped into the girls' room.

Empty. Quiet. Perfect.

I was just about to flush when I heard other girls coming into the bathroom. I quietly took my hand off the flusher when I realized those girls were Elena Maxwell's Gang of 3.

The Gang of 3 are:

1. Sissy Mendez. Her mom, Mrs. Mendez, is another fifth-grade teacher. Sissy and Elena have been best friends since preschool. She once scared Augustus Sawyer so much that he climbed a tree and wouldn't come down for twelve hours. Also, she's very tall.
2. Chloe Martin. When we were in kindergarten, Chloe made a crown of daisies for me. She put it on my head and held my hand and said we would be best friends forever. I don't think she knew what *forever* meant because last time I saw her she poured Jell-O in my book bag.
3. Elena Maxwell. The leader and, as I stated earlier, my nemesis.

The feud between Elena and me began in second grade when I refused to join her gang. I did not like the idea of her bossing me around, and she did not like the idea of me not liking it. So she bossed me into the janitor's closet and locked me inside. It took all of recess and lunch for Mr. Dale, the janitor, to find me and let me out.

It's what happened after the janitor's closet that caused

the problem. I'm not very forgiving. Atticus tells me it is a character flaw and I need to work on it. I tell Atticus he's never been locked in a janitor's closet.

I had one of my grand ideas. I have a grand idea every few months and this one happened to strike just seconds after Mr. Dale let me out of the closet.

Marcus Johnson was a kid in our class who could not keep his fingers out of his nose. Elena sat next to Marcus and couldn't stand him. "Mrs. Greene," she would say, raising her hand so high you would think she was hailing a taxi, "Mrs. Greene, he's doing it again!"

Everyone in Mrs. Greene's second-grade class would turn and look at Marcus, who of course had one finger sticking up a runny nostril.

I liked Marcus and he owed me a favor. So, the next day, on my cue, Marcus walked up behind Elena at recess. I called her name and she turned around. Marcus and Elena were exactly the same height in second grade. And his lips were ready.

Marcus didn't have to do a thing. They were lip-to-lip before Elena knew what hit her.

While Elena was screaming and wiping her mouth on her sleeve, I walked up to Marcus, shook his snotty hand, and said thank you. Then I smiled at Elena.

The feud has raged ever since. Third grade. Fourth grade. Almost three years.

And now, here I was, trapped in a toilet stall with Elena

and her minions outside. Quietly, I pulled my feet up onto the toilet seat. What else was I supposed to do? There were three of them and only one of me. So I did what any sane person trapped in a girls' room stall would do. I sat there and listened.

Elena, Sissy, and Chloe talked and talked. They talked about boys. They talked about nail polish. They talked about whose hair was longer and shinier. I was about to go numb with boredom when they started talking about me.

"Did you see Avalon?" Elena suddenly said. "Those shoes are ridiculous. It's like she was raised by wolves or something."

"Fashion-deprived wolves," Chloe said, and laughed.

I looked down at my lime-green saddle shoes, perched on the toilet seat. Fashion deprived? I wasn't the one who wore white pants with American flag underwear.

"I'm finally going to get back at her for that picture she took of me!" Elena exclaimed. "It was so unfair!"

Unfair? Was she kidding? Who does she think filled my cubby with green slime? Or pasted the pages of my math book together? Or taped strips of toilet paper to the bottom of my shoes? Or locked me in a janitor's closet?!

"Avalon thinks she can get away with everything," Elena continued. "Well, we'll just see about that."

"I put Jell-O in her book bag," said Chloe.

"That's not enough!" Elena snarled loudly. I wondered if Cruella or Maleficent got their start this way.

"This is what we're going to do," Elena said, and started to unveil the details of her evil plan. Unfortunately, for dramatic effect, she decided to unveil them in a whisper, which meant I couldn't hear. But eventually she got so pleased with herself that her voice got louder again. "Avalon's so stupid," I heard her say. "She'll never see it coming. And no one can ever know. We just have to act normal. That means you two. Got it?!"

I could practically see Sissy and Chloe nodding through the bathroom stall door.

Sissy giggled. "She'll have no idea what hit her."

"Deal?" Elena said.

"Deal," said Sissy and Chloe together. Then I heard the clap of hands.

I was staring at my saddle shoes when I heard the girls' room door slam behind them as they left. Something bad was going to happen. Something big. I needed to tell Atticus.

By the time I made it to the fifth-grade hallway, my mind was filled with thoughts of Elena and what terrible things she could do to me. It never occurred to me that something even more terrible was about to unfold.

Atticus was leaning against the wall outside of Ms. Smith's classroom. I hurried toward him. "You're never going to believe what just happened," I said, all out of breath, collapsing against the wall beside him. "You were right. Elena's planning to get back at me for the picture I took. They're going to do something really bad to me but I couldn't hear what it was. Elena sounds even crazier and meaner than usual." I looked around. All the kids had gone back to the auditorium. But I started whispering anyway. "I'm so glad we are going to have our Infinity Year powers. I think we might really need them. Like *need them*, need them." As I paused to think about that, a more frightening thought exploded in my head. "What if Elena, Chloe, and Sissy get them, too?! What if they get Infinity Year powers! That would be horrible! Think about how much worse Elena would be if she actually had magical powers!"

I turned my head toward Atticus but he wasn't looking at me. I'm not sure he was even listening. "Do you hear what I'm saying?" I asked. "This is serious."

"So is this," Atticus said.

He was staring at the opposite wall. He hadn't looked at me yet. What could possibly be more serious than what I was telling him? "You know how we thought we'd be in Ms. Smith's class?" he said.

"Yeah," I answered.

Atticus looked at me. "Well, we're not."

"Oh," I said. "Okay." I felt a tingle run up the back of my neck. "What class are we in then?"

"Avie, you don't understand. *I'm* in Ms. Smith's class."

"What?!" I turned to the list posted on Ms. Smith's door. I read down it as fast as I could. No Avalon James on that list. I looked at Atticus. He nodded toward the room next door.

Mrs. Jackson's class. Mrs. Jackson, who has been teaching for about 110 years. There was no laughter in Mrs. Jackson's class. There was, however, a long whisker growing out of a mole on Mrs. Jackson's chin.

I was in Mrs. Jackson's class.

But that wasn't the worst of it. There were other names on that list, too. Martin . . . Maxwell . . . Mendez. I was going to be in the same class with Elena, Sissy, and Chloe. The last time we were all in the same class was in second grade. And look how well that turned out.

That evil threesome was going to be with me every day, everywhere. Even when we went to lunch.

Atticus tried to cheer me up. "At least we'll have recess together."

I looked at him sideways. "Great," I said, and slid down the wall. Atticus looked down at me and then sat down beside me.

We sat there for a long time and didn't say a word. This was more serious than Elena and her stupid plan. This was about me and Atticus. How could this have happened?

Atticus nudged his knee against mine. "So what if Elena has a plan. She's had tons of plans. And she's not going to get an Infinity Year power. That only happens between best friends." He knocked my knee again. "And you know Chloe will tell somebody. Whatever Elena is planning, Chloe will tell," he said. "She can't keep a secret."

"She can keep an Elena secret," I said. "She's too scared of her."

"See what I mean. Best friends are not scared of each other. So they're not best friends. You know what that means?"

"No. What?"

"We will be getting our Infinity Year powers," Atticus said, and then grinned. "And Elena Maxwell will not."

The night of the open house, I couldn't sleep. Mostly because of the shock of Atticus and me not being in the same class. But something else was bothering me, too. It was this thing between me and Elena. It had been going on for so long. Sure, she started it. But I'd never been able to end it. I might not be the kind of person who can just let things go.

Sometimes I wished I were that kind of person, though. Sometimes I wished I could travel back in time and take back that kiss I made Marcus give Elena. If I could just take back his snotty handshake and my big fat smile, Elena might have moved on to torture some other undeserving soul. At least that's what Atticus always said.

M was purring and curled up beside me. I curled in closer. None of it mattered now. I was going to be alone with Elena in Mrs. Jackson's class and that was that.

I turned over and M meowed.

Meowed. M-E-O-W-E-D. I spelled it in my head. Meowed.

Hmmm. Maybe there could be an upside to being in Mrs. Jackson's class, even if Atticus wasn't going to be with me. The thing about Mrs. Jackson was that, as well as being a fifth-grade teacher, she was also the faculty sponsor for the School-Wide Spelling Bee.

Some people were good at lots of things. Atticus was good at soccer, comic book reading, and *Titanic* trivia. Mae Bearman was good at gymnastics, drawing, and hula hooping. Adam Singleton could hold his breath for sixty-five seconds underwater and spit over twelve and a half feet.

I was good at one thing.

Spelling.

It's something I got from my dad. He was a spelling champ when he was in school. They said he had great potential.

He realized I had the gift when I was five. My mom asked how to spell *kangaroo* and I spelled it before he did. After that, he pulled out his old spelling books and gave them to me. We used to practice whenever he could find time.

In my school, you had to be in fourth grade to enter the school's spelling bee. Waiting to be in fourth grade took forever. Infinity, in fact. When I finally got there, I thought I was ready. But fourth grade turned out to be a very unlucky year for me.

This year was going to be different. Even if I still had Elena to deal with. Because this was my Infinity Year. And somehow, someway, I had the feeling something good was supposed to happen.

After all, the school spelling bee was in January. And I had been preparing for it my entire life.

TWO

On the first day of fifth grade, Mrs. Brightwell drove up to our house at 7:30 sharp. From my bedroom window, I saw Atticus get out of her car and dump his backpack next to our mailbox.

"Mom! They're here!" I yelled, and kissed M, who was still sleeping on our bed. "I don't have lunch money!"

I walked into my mom's bedroom. She was dressed in her robe and putting on makeup.

"Mom! I'm gonna be late," I said.

"You and me both," she said, and flung her purse across the bed. "Just get what you need."

I dug into my mom's big yellow wallet and came up with a five-dollar bill. "Can I take this?" I held up the bill as if for inspection.

"Sure," she said. I tucked it in my pocket and turned to leave. "But bring the change."

"Okay," I said, and picked up my backpack in the hallway.

"Have a good day," Mom called out. "And remember you're going to Mrs. White's after school."

"I know," I yelled back, and slipped out the door.

Atticus was waiting for me at the end of our driveway. He wasn't alone. Mrs. Brightwell was still there. She had rolled down the window of her car and was looking at Atticus like he was a beloved dog she was leaving at the pound.

"Are you sure I can't follow you?" she asked as I walked up beside him.

"Mom, you promised," Atticus said. "We'll be fine."

"But—"

"It's okay," he said. "School's just down the street."

"Could I at least pick you up after school with everyone else?" she asked.

"Mom!" Atticus exclaimed.

"Okay, okay," she said. "I'll pick you up here."

"Mrs. White's," I chimed in.

Mrs. Brightwell looked next door. "Mrs. White's," she said, exasperated. "What time?"

"About four thirty?" Atticus said, looking at me for confirmation.

I nodded.

Mrs. Brightwell sighed.

Atticus's mom does not like me. Atticus tells me that's

not true and that his mom likes me fine. Unlike him, I have a little thing called women's intuition and it tells me that he is dead wrong. If I had a nickel for every time Mrs. Brightwell has rolled her eyes or sighed when Atticus mentioned my name, I'd be a hundredaire by now.

As Mrs. Brightwell drove away, Atticus and I picked up our backpacks and started walking.

I never liked the first day of school but this was definitely the worst First Day ever. Atticus and I would be in separate classes. I was going to be trapped in old Mrs. Jackson's class with Cruella and her evil stepsisters. And this was the first First Day my dad wasn't walking me to school.

We didn't talk as we walked past Mrs. White's house, where every bird in the neighborhood was gathered at the big bird feeder outside her kitchen window. When I'm doing my homework at her kitchen table after school, she likes to whistle to them while she makes me a snack. Mrs. White loves her birds. M hates them.

"Atticus, I've been thinking about something," I said as we left Mrs. White's house behind. "I've been thinking about where we're going to go when we grow up and leave this place."

"Where do you want to go?" he asked.

"The Galápagos Islands. For starters."

"Okay," Atticus said.

"Tell me about the ocean again."

Atticus knows that talking about the ocean soothes me. It

is one of my true-life aims to see it one day. Atticus has seen the ocean many times. His family goes there every summer.

"It's bigger than you'd think," he said. "And it's loud. Like a constant roar. All day and all night. It's cold, too. Whenever I get in and it's cold like that, I always think about how cold it must have been." He shook his head. "You know. On that night."

"That night" was the night the *Titanic* sank. Atticus is a freak about the *Titanic*. He knows everything about it. Everything. If you don't already know, the *Titanic* was a ship that was supposed to be unsinkable. On its first voyage, however, it sank in the middle of the ocean, in the middle of the night. It happened over a hundred years ago and lots of people died and Atticus is totally obsessed with it—to the point where I think it might be unhealthy.

I shrugged my shoulders. The ocean the *Titanic* sank in was not the kind of ocean I was thinking about. "I don't care what it looks like at night."

"But you should, Avie. The ocean's beautiful at night. It goes on forever and ever. To infinity."

"Infinity," I said quietly.

We walked for a minute without talking. I was careful not to step on any cracks in the sidewalk. I'd had enough bad luck already.

"Did you talk to your mom about what Elena said?" Atticus asked.

"No," I answered.

"Why not?"

"You know. Like she needs one more thing to worry about."

"Yeah," he said, and kicked a stone across the sidewalk.

Ever since last year, Mom's been working as a nurse again. She used to be a nurse before I was born but quit working after that so she could take care of me. Now she was back in the ICU at St. Joseph's. She works long hours and she's tired a lot.

"But I've got a plan," I said.

"What plan?"

I smiled. "I'm going to cut off Elena's ponytail and feed it to the tigers."

He stopped and looked at me. "Seriously?"

"Seriously," I said. "We're going to the zoo this year."

"That's months away."

"So."

"I'm not in your class, Avie," Atticus said. "And she is."

"It'll be okay," I lied. "I can take care of myself."

"Right."

We started walking again. Atticus knew me. He knew I was the kind of person who really would cut off someone's ponytail if it came to it. He also knew that his voice was always in the back of my head telling me that cutting off ponytails was a bad idea. Most of the time, the voice of Atticus would win.

Sometimes it would not.

I could see the school up ahead beyond the mailbox at the top of our street. Once a week, I put a letter into that mailbox. Today was one of those days. I pulled an envelope from my backpack and slipped it through the slot.

"I ran into Chloe at the mall last weekend," I said. "And it went okay." I neglected to mention the Jell-O incident.

"I'll be just next door," he said. "If you need anything."

I smiled inside.

"I mean it, Avie."

"I know," I said.

The crossing guard stopped traffic in front of us. The walk was over. Time to cross the street and start fifth grade.

I turned and saw Mrs. Brightwell parked in the lot next to the Jiffy Freeze, right across the street from school. The Jiffy Freeze has the best double chocolate fudge ice cream cones in town. Our eyes met. I could tell she didn't think we were going to see her. She was so busted.

I quickly turned away. Atticus didn't know his mother would spy on him. But I did. He deserved to know.

I looked back toward the Jiffy Freeze. Mrs. Brightwell had disappeared. Her car was still there but she wasn't. I would bet my bowl of Seashells of the World that she was ducking beneath the dashboard.

Today, I decided to let the voice of Atticus in my head win. I followed him across the street feeling the eyes of Mrs. Brightwell burning a hole in my back every step of the way.

She would owe me for this.

Atticus walked me to my class and wished me luck. I looked inside and saw Elena's Gang of 3 staring back at me.

Mrs. Jackson sat us in alphabetical order, so my desk happened to be next to Chloe Martin's. In the desk behind Chloe was Elena Maxwell and in the desk behind Elena was Sissy Mendez.

Alphabetical order can really stink.

Marcus Johnson sat behind me and, like in second grade, his desk was right beside Elena's. She looked over at Marcus as if she couldn't believe this was happening to her again. In response, Marcus puckered his lips and blew her an air-kiss. Elena dramatically threw her hands to her face and groaned.

Mrs. Jackson stood up from behind her desk and wrote her name in big letters on the chalkboard. I thought that was funny. Who in this class didn't already know that she was Mrs. Jackson?

She started by telling us all the rules of her classroom. Like how we shouldn't run or chew gum or speak without raising our hands. I stared at the long whisker growing out of her chin. It wiggled with every word she said.

"There is one last rule of this classroom that must be abided by above all others," Mrs. Jackson continued. As she spoke she wrote this in big letters under her name:

NO BULLIES ALLOWED

She suddenly had my attention.

"There will be no bullying in this class," she said. "Anyone who exhibits bullying behavior will be sent directly to Mr. Peterson's office."

I turned and looked at Elena. She acted like she didn't see me but I knew she did.

That would be great if Elena was sent to Mr. Peterson's office. That would really make my Infinity Year.

Mr. Peterson was the kind of principal who told jokes to the students and dressed up on Halloween but if you had to go to his office, it was a different story altogether. Last year, Adam Singleton hocked a loogie onto the chalkboard right in the middle of our math class. It was gross. Ms. Kinney sent him directly to Mr. Peterson's office. He didn't come back until after recess and I could tell he had been crying. Ever since, I have wondered what Mr. Peterson did to him. Adam wouldn't tell.

I figured if Mr. Peterson can make Adam Singleton cry, he might have a chance with Elena.

At that moment, a grand idea sprang forth. I didn't have to do anything to Elena this year. She would do it to herself. All I had to do was be sure Mrs. Jackson was watching when Elena struck.

I could do that.

THREE

It was the third week of school when I bumped into Harinder Singh.

It was Pizza Friday and Mae Bearman and I were going through the lunch line. Mae and I were teaming up quite a bit these days. Mrs. Jackson assigned us to be partners in our Family Tree Project. Then, in recess, Mae shared her jump rope with me while Atticus was playing kickball. Now, every day Mae lets the *C*s through the *I*s pass her in the lunch line so we can get our lunches together.

So we were in the lunch line and Mae was talking all about how her grandmother has these pictures of old dead people we can put on her family tree. I listened and smiled at the lunch ladies while Mae talked.

We both chose a cheese slice with peas on the side and a

carton of milk. I enjoy Pizza Friday. It's the one day when lunchroom food tastes almost like the real thing.

I picked up my tray and started walking into the lunchroom. I was ahead of Mae because she went back to switch her regular milk for the strawberry kind (which is so disgusting). All the fifth and the seventh graders share the same lunch period and Mrs. Jackson's class is one of the last to arrive, so you can imagine how crowded and loud it was in there.

Mae said something to me from behind. I couldn't hear her so I turned around.

"See you after lunch," she said loudly, and nodded toward the middle of our table. Each class has to sit at the same long table at lunch. Mae usually sits in the middle of the Mrs. Jackson table so she can lean across the aisle and talk to her best friend, Hannah, who sits at the Mrs. Mendez table.

"Okay," I said, and turned back around.

That's when I collided with Harinder Singh. My lunch tray went flying. Pizza went one way and green peas went every other way. The tray hit the tile floor and bounced really loud. The lunchroom went totally silent.

Everybody was looking at me.

I have a habit of opening my milk in the lunch line and taking a sip. Now I know why the lunch ladies frown upon this practice. Milk was in my hair, in my eyes, all over my shirt, and dripping down my neck. A white pool was forming around my feet. It wasn't funny. But apparently the entire fifth and seventh grades of Grover Cleveland K–8 School didn't agree. They all started laughing.

I quickly bent down to pick up my tray.

"Are you all right?"

I looked up. Harinder was kneeling beside me.

"I'm sorry," he said. "I didn't see you there." He picked up my tray and disappeared. There I remained, covered in milk, alone, in the middle of the lunchroom. Oh, the joys of fifth grade. Note to self: Infinity Year powers DO NOT help with spilled milk in laughing lunchrooms.

It took what seemed like an embarrassingly long time before Harinder came back with two kitchen towels.

"Thanks," I said, and took the towels.

Everyone was still laughing and watching me while I started to wipe milk from my face. Harinder noticed and turned to the room. "What are you looking at?" he said loudly, with all the authority of a seventh grader.

The whole lunchroom got quiet. I watched in awe as they turned away and went back to their pizzas and peas.

"I'm Hari, by the way," he said.

I knew that. Everybody knows who Hari Singh is. His real name is Harinder but all the kids call him Hari. He is tall with dark hair that droops over one eye and his nose is a little bit crooked. But that's not what matters. What matters is that Hari Singh is the current spelling champion of our school.

He must have noticed I was staring.

"Are those your flashcards?" he asked.

I looked behind me. My flashcards had fallen out of the bag that I carry to lunch. Other than M, my flashcards are my most important things. I take them almost everywhere. You never know when there'll be a spare moment to learn a new word.

"You're a speller?" he asked.

"Yeah," I answered.

"Awesome."

He gave me a little grin while two lunch ladies and Mrs. Mendez approached to help clean up the mess—which included me.

I watched him walk back to one of the seventh-grade tables. Harinder Singh—who went to the National Spelling Bee last spring. Harinder Singh—who, out of 289 participants, came in twenty-seventh of all the kids in the whole country. M and I watched the whole thing on TV.

"Avie?"

I turned and saw Atticus standing beside me.

"I was in the bathroom," he said. "What happened?"

Atticus has to pee more than any other human I know. He'll do it anywhere, too. No bathroom required.

"Come on, Avalon," Mrs. Mendez said. "Let's get you some fresh clothes."

While Mrs. Mendez led me toward the lunchroom door,

I looked back at Atticus. "My flashcards," I mouthed. He looked down and saw them, so I knew it would be all right.

We passed Elena, Chloe, and Sissy, who were sitting at one end of the Mrs. Jackson table.

"Look at the Milk Monster," Sissy said, and laughed. Elena's eyes met mine as she leaned over to Sissy and whispered something in her ear. I watched as Sissy's eyes got wide and her head started nodding madly. Elena was clearly adding a new twist to the already diabolical plan they had in store for me.

Sissy's mother, whose claw was biting into my shoulder, did nothing but smile.

Mrs. Mendez dropped me off at the nurse's office as if I had a head full of lice or something. She couldn't get away from me fast enough.

Nurse Davis was really nice, though. She sat me on the exam table and helped me take off my milky shoes. She said she would clean them up while I was in the shower.

While I showered in the little bathroom off the nurse's office, I thought about my Infinity Year power. I had been focusing very hard on it ever since school began. What would it be? When would it show up? I hadn't told Atticus yet but there'd been a couple of times—always when it was really quiet at night and there was just me and M—that I'd started to feel . . . something. Something deep down inside. Like the magic was hovering somewhere, ready to come through. And just because it hadn't shown up to help me in the lunchroom didn't mean it wasn't real. Maybe it just wasn't ready. Maybe it was saving itself for when I needed it most. Maybe one day my Infinity Year power was going to erupt like one of Ms. Smith's volcanoes and save the day.

Ten minutes later I was back in the lunchroom at the opposite end of the table from Elena, Chloe, and Sissy, wearing a *Be a Reading Geek* T-shirt.

Sitting right next to Atticus.

We worked it out the very first day of school. The Mrs. Jackson table is between the Mrs. Mendez and Ms. Smith tables. Ms. Smith's class gets to lunch before us, so Atticus sits at the end of their table and doesn't let anyone sit in the chair next to him at our table. Until I arrive.

No one sits in our seats. Everyone knows those seats are reserved for Avalon and Atticus.

Adam Singleton and Kevin Matthews always sit next to Atticus at their table. Sometimes Eva Chang sits next to me—that's when she's not sitting with Amy Atkins-McGregor.

On this day, it was just me and the boys. As I sat down, Atticus handed me my flashcards and one of the lunch ladies, Miss Judy, brought me a replacement lunch. "Be careful with this one," she said as she gave me a milk carton.

I half smiled until she turned away. "Why does stuff like this happen to me?" I groaned.

"'Member that time you went to the blackboard and your

dress was stuck all up into your underwear?" Adam said like it was a great moment in history. I remember it as the last day I ever wore a dress to class.

"Or how about that time you fell asleep on your desk and woke up with a Magic Marker mustache," Kevin added.

"Oh, yeah! And remember when you got locked in the janitor's closet?" Adam said. "That was hilari—"

He broke off. I turned just in time to see the arch in Atticus's left eyebrow come down. He had a way of silencing people with that eyebrow of his.

"A lot of that wasn't my fault," I said.

"Course it wasn't," Atticus said. Then, without missing a beat, "Did you guys realize we haven't even started talking about Halloween yet?"

"What should we go as?" Adam said excitedly.

"Thor or Iron Man," Kevin answered.

"Everybody goes as them!" Adam said. "I'm going as Ant-Man. Ant-Man has a cybernetic helmet."

"So," Kevin said louder. "Iron Man has a body helmet."

"So . . ."

And it continued. The ongoing argument about who was the most awesomely supreme Avenger. Atticus was a genius.

I looked up at the clock on the wall. It was 12:24. Almost time to go back to class. I took a couple of bites of pizza. Gobbled down some peas. Had a few spoonfuls of Jell-O (Miss Judy had brought me some cherry Jell-O, too!).

Atticus picked up his tray. "See you at recess."

"Okay." I nodded. After lunch, we go back to our class-rooms for thirty minutes of reading, followed by science for Atticus and English for me. Then comes my favorite forty minutes of the day. Recess.

I watched Atticus and the boys line up to go back to Ms. Smith's class. I still had a few minutes before our line formed.

I pulled out my flashcards and looked at these words:

Harbinger

Petticoat

Satisfaction

A black cat crossed the road in front of me, which is a harbinger of bad things to come. I drew up my petticoat as I stepped over a puddle. When I slipped and fell into the puddle anyway, the cat turned and looked at me with satisfaction.

Making sentences with words helps my brain remember how to spell them. Words are like math to me. They make sense.

I looked down at the other end of the table at Chloe, Sissy, and Elena. Other than the Milk Monster comment, the three of them had been suspiciously good so far this year. If I hadn't overheard them in the bathroom, I would probably feel pretty relaxed right about then. I'd be thinking that Mrs. Jackson's no-bullying policy was actually working.

Of course, I'd be wrong.

We walked back to Mrs. Jackson's class in single file. While Marcus Johnson tried to step on the back of my sneakers, I thought about Halloween. Me and Atticus went as Peter Pan and Tinker Bell last year. Adam went as Captain Hook and Kevin dressed up like the Crocodile. That kind of Halloween was over. I wasn't going to be able to talk them into being Disney characters anymore. Fifth-grade boys wanted to be superheroes and villains with more than hook hands and massive teeth. I wondered what fifth-grade girls wanted to be.

When we got back to class, I went to get a book from the library in the back of our classroom and picked up *Charlotte's Web*. I've always had a soft spot for pigs and spiders. Just like my mom. This was her favorite book when she was a kid. She used to read it to me some nights when my dad was working late. We'd snuggle up with M between us and read about Charlotte and Wilbur.

Other than the milk incident, the day was turning out to be okay. Maybe even magical. After all, I'd met Hari Singh. He actually spoke to me. He knows I'm a speller. And he thought that was awesome.

I even found myself smiling at Elena as I went to my desk. Until I sat down into what felt like a pool of Jell-O.

Great. Great. Triple great.

I stood up enough to see what it actually was. And yes, it was cherry Jell-O. My jeans were soaked with it.

I looked over at Elena. She was smiling at me now. Elena had big brown eyes and long black curly hair. She wore the newest clothes, carried the nicest book bag, and always had perfectly painted nails. If that look of meanness hadn't already spoiled her face, Elena Maxwell might actually be pretty.

Her eyes narrowed like she was daring me to tell Mrs. Jackson.

The Jell-O I was sitting in wasn't the big mean thing they were planning. I had had enough clods of dirt in my pockets and broken pencils in my pencil box to know that. This was only an appetizer on Elena's menu of meanness. The main course was still to come.

I looked over at Mrs. Jackson. Telling her would have been an option. But Elena would have just denied it and then everyone would know I had Jell-O all over my jeans.

I sat back down with a squish. Elena Maxwell would not get the best of me today.

As my butt began to chill, I remembered Atticus warning me not to post the picture of Elena and her American flag underwear on the bulletin board. But it was fabulous and I hadn't been able to stop myself.

Plus, Elena had been mean to me in fourth grade. Really mean. She deserved it.

"Don't let her know she gets to you," Atticus was always saying. But she really gets to me. Sometimes I just want to punch her in the face.

When we were in the same class, I could look at Atticus and, usually, that would calm me down. But this year Atticus was in the room next door, which might as well have been in China. I was alone with the devil herself.

It was going to be a very long year.

FOUR

Atticus is a vegetarian and it drives Mrs. Brightwell crazy. She will feed me the most delicious hamburger right in front of him in hopes that he will give in and ask for one.

He never does.

Atticus can't believe that I let his mother use me like this.

I can't believe that he misses out on such great burgers.

Atticus quit eating meat of any kind in third grade. I remember when it happened. It was during a weekend at his grandparents' farm. His Granny and Pop-pop have a farm outside of town where they raise cattle and grow strawberries.

Atticus loves animals and he had named every cow in their herd. He helped raise one of the calves after the calf's mom died. He named the calf Frank, and Atticus would bottle-feed Frank and play with him every weekend. I met Frank on several occasions and have to say that Frank (despite his name) was pretty adorable.

His Pop-pop always told Atticus not to get attached to the animals, and that weekend at lunch, Atticus asked why.

Pop-pop pointed with a fork at the hamburger Atticus was eating and said, "Because that's what Frank's going to grow up to be one day."

Atticus put down his hamburger, left the table, and never ate a piece of meat again.

We hadn't been to the farm since fifth grade started. I got up early on the third Saturday morning in September because Atticus and I were going for the whole day.

I woke up before my mom and tiptoed into her room. She still slept on her side of the bed. The other side of the bed looked lonely and sad. Mom had worked late at the hospital the night before and picked me up at Mrs. White's house. I had fallen asleep on Mrs. White's couch and barely remembered getting home.

I got dressed, ate a bowl of cereal all by myself, then waited in front of my window for Mrs. Brightwell's car to drive up. M jumped onto my lap and we looked out into the neighborhood. It was so quiet out there. Like everyone was still asleep, just like my mom.

I reached for the conch shell that was sitting on my

windowsill and held it up to my ear. It was a gift from Atticus from one of his family's summer trips to the beach. They say you're supposed to hear the ocean in that little shell. I listened hard but if there's an ocean in there it must be a thousand miles away. I listened harder. I imagined the waves. Atticus always said how loud they were. I strained to hear them in my head.

Mrs. Brightwell's car pulled into our driveway. I put M on our bed and kissed her right between her ears. "Have a good day, M," I said even though I knew she would miss me.

I grabbed my backpack and looked inside. Mom had put an extra sweatshirt in there along with my flashcards. I carried it with me as I stepped into her room again. She was still sound asleep.

"Mom," I whispered.

"What?" she answered instantly, the way moms do.

"They're here."

"Oh, okay." She sat up and looked at me. "You got everything?"

I held up my backpack.

"Did you eat?" she asked, rubbing her eyes.

"Fruity Pebbles."

"Oh, great."

"Fruity *and* nutritious," I said, and smiled at her.

Mom shook her head. She was always trying to get me to eat healthy cereals. But she still bought me the ones I liked.

"Have fun," she said, and held out her arm to me. I walked over and she gave me a little squeeze.

"I will," I said. As I turned toward the door, I could feel her falling asleep again.

I slipped out the side door that led to the garage and locked it behind me. Then I ran down the driveway to Mrs. Brightwell's car. I got in the backseat next to Atticus.

Atticus's sister, Caroline, was sitting in the front seat next to Mrs. Brightwell. Caroline has long red hair, green eyes, and perfectly perfect teeth. Her boyfriend, Will, is on the football team and Caroline is a cheerleader.

Caroline has lots of friends and always seems to be smiling. We have nothing in common but I have to like Caroline because she likes Atticus just about as much as I do.

As I shut the door to the car, I heard Mrs. Brightwell say, "That's enough of this for now," in a tone that said no more talking about whatever it was they had been talking about in front of me.

"Good morning, Avalon," she then said brightly.

"Hi, Mrs. Brightwell," I said as I buckled my seat belt. "Hi, Caroline." I looked at Atticus. I could tell something was bothering him.

Mrs. Brightwell was going to drop us at the farm and then she and Mr. Brightwell were going to visit his younger sister, who'd just had a baby girl. Atticus's Aunt Lori and Uncle Kevin already had one kid, Atticus's cousin Michael.

Whenever they'd visit in the summer or at Christmas, we'd let Michael hang out with us even though he was a year younger. This last summer, though, Michael had gotten so tall that Atticus and I looked like the littler kids. It didn't bother Atticus until Michael started teasing him, calling him "little cuz" and holding a football way over Atticus's head. Atticus jumped for it once but then just gave up and went inside.

I looked at Michael real hard. That's all it took. He gave me the football. But I didn't feel so good about Michael after that.

"What do you squirts want to do today?" Caroline asked. She turned to us, draping her arm over the front seat.

Atticus shrugged.

Yes, something was definitely wrong.

"Come on, Atti." She reached back and jiggled his knee. "Come on, it's gonna be fun. We'll do whatever you want."

This was strange. Usually when we go to the farm under Caroline's supervision, me and Atticus take off and do whatever we want while Caroline texts her friends from the farmhouse.

"Come on!" she pleaded loudly and made a funny face.

"Caroline!" Mrs. Brightwell said. "Leave your brother alone."

"I can't," she said, and put on a pouty voice. "He's my dreamy dreamboat. My dreamiest dreamboat. Of all the dreamy dreamboats." She batted her eyes at him.

Atticus could never resist Caroline. He started to smile.

Fifteen minutes later we were at the farmhouse. As we got out of the car, Pop-pop came out to meet us in the driveway. He held out his hand to me and said, "Give me five, sprout." He has greeted me in this way since I was six.

I gave him five and he pretended to almost fall over from the force of my hand. This, too, he has done since I was six.

"Hey, cowboy," he said to Atticus, and they both pulled imaginary guns out of imaginary holsters and pointed them at each other. Yeah. Since six.

"And if you get more beautiful, my eyeballs are going to pop out," he said to Caroline.

"Ah, Pop-pop," she said, hugging her grandfather.

"We'll be back to get them by seven," Mrs. Brightwell said. "Seven thirty at the latest." She pecked her father on the cheek and waved to her mother, who had stepped out onto the porch.

"Why don't you let the children stay overnight?" Pop-pop said. "I'll tell them ghost stories that'll turn their hair gray."

Atticus and I swung around hopefully to Mrs. Brightwell, but she was already shaking her head. "Not tonight," she said. "Maybe some other time." We could've moaned and pleaded but we knew it wouldn't change things.

As she pulled out of the driveway, Pop-pop looked at Atticus. "Your mother may be my daughter, but I got to say, sometimes I think that girl has lost her fun."

He turned to me. "F-U-N," he spelled. "Fun." He grinned and clapped his hands together.

I laughed. Pop-pop can be funny.

Sometimes.

But Pop-pop can be serious, too. He grew up on the farm, and he'd sometimes tell us super-serious stories about weird things that happened when he was a boy. Like when his brother shot an arrow straight up in the air and watched it come all the way back down and land right between his eyes. (Don't worry, he lived.) Or the time Pop-pop caught the top of his uncle's index finger when it accidentally got cut off in the old sawmill.

Or when he got his magical power during his Infinity Year.

Yep. That's how we know about the Infinity Year. Atticus's grandfather is the reliable source who told us about it in the first place.

It was right before Atticus's birthday last year. We were sitting on the tailgate of the truck in the pasture watching after a cow, who was about to have a baby cow. It takes a long time sometimes for a cow to be born so we were talking to Pop-pop and keeping him company.

I remember Pop-pop was chewing on a piece of hay. We were pointing out shapes in the big fluffy clouds that filled the sky that day. Yawning dogs, puffy hats, and battleships all floated by as we talked.

At first, I thought Pop-pop was kidding when he started telling us about how our Infinity Year was coming up. Pop-pop has been known to tell a tall tale or two. But there was something different about this. About the way he told us. He was serious.

It started way back, a very long time ago, when Pop-pop was about to turn ten. It was a spring day and Pop-pop and his friend Jimmy Riggins were at his grandfather's house late one afternoon. Pop-pop and Jimmy were best friends. Probably kind of like me and Atticus.

"There was a tornado coming through," Pop-pop said, "and we all went down into the root cellar."

"What's a root cellar?" I asked.

"A place underground. Where we kept the root vegetables during the winter. Didn't you ever see *The Wizard of Oz*?" he asked.

Atticus and I both nodded.

"It was in the root cellar that my Grandpa Daniel told us about the time back when he was ten and he and his best friend got their magical powers."

"What magical powers?" Atticus asked, his eyes little round saucers.

"Grandpa Daniel could become invisible whenever he wanted," Pop-pop said. "And his friend could outrun any horse on the farm."

"No," we said together.

"Yes." Pop-pop nodded. "But those powers went away on the day they turned eleven."

"You're kidding," I said. "That's impossible."

"Is it?" Pop-pop answered, raising his eyebrow just like Atticus does.

"Did it happen to you, Pop-pop?" Atticus suddenly asked. "Did you and Jimmy get your magical powers?"

Pop-pop grinned and looked us both straight in the eyes. "We did. We sure did."

"What were they?" Atticus yelled.

"Tell us!" I pleaded, too.

"Shhhh." Pop-pop put a finger to his lips and looked toward the mama cow, who was still thinking about having her baby. "I'll tell you about that when you're eleven. Something to look forward to," he said, and grinned. "But just remember, you can't talk about it with anybody else. Not with any of your other friends. That's the rule. It has to be a secret. Between true best friends. That's the only way the magic happens. That's why I had to tell it to the two of you."

Atticus and I looked at each other. Both of our mouths were wide open.

Atticus turned back to his grandpa. "Why does it happen when you're ten?" he asked. I thought that was kind of a silly question—who cares *why* it happens as long as it *happens*— but Pop-pop looked thoughtful, like it deserved a serious answer.

"No one can really say, cowboy," he said, and looked up to

the sky. "But the way I figure it is this. When you're ten years old, your life's really starting to open up. It's just kind of a special time, a magical time when anything can happen, where the possibilities are endless."

He brushed his hand over both of our heads. "The possibilities are endless," he repeated. "Infinite. That's why we called it the Infinity Year. Least, Jimmy did. He was like you, sprout. Loved his big words. I-N-F-I-N-I-T-Y. Infinity."

"Tell us one thing about your power, Pop-pop," Atticus begged. "Please."

"Okay," he said. "One thing only." He looked around as if to make sure nobody else could hear. "Your magical power can come in one of two ways. Like my Grandpa Daniel, it can be a power you can call on time and time again. Or it can be a power that comes only once—when you need it most."

"Is that what happened to you?" I asked.

"You got it when you needed it most?" Atticus asked.

He winked at us then he hopped off the tailgate. "We'll talk about it when you're eleven," he said, and walked over toward the cow.

That was last spring, and so far, Pop-pop has kept his word and has never talked about it, no matter how much we've begged. He's only said that we'll talk about it afterward. When our Infinity Year is done.

This drives Atticus and me crazy.

After Mrs. Brightwell drove off, Atticus, Caroline, and I

followed Pop-pop into the farmhouse. Inside, Granny was standing in front of the griddle making pancakes and bacon for breakfast.

Caroline and Atticus went to hug their grandmother as I sat down at the kitchen table.

"Morning, Avalon," she called out over the sizzle of the griddle. "You want Atticus's bacon?"

I nodded enthusiastically. "Yes, please!" She brought me a plate piled high with pancakes and bacon. I didn't tell her about the Fruity Pebbles.

"Bacon, bacon," she said, and kissed Atticus on the top of the head. "You don't know what you're missing, boy." The bacon *was* delicious. So delicious I forgot about Wilbur altogether.

As we ate and everyone was talking around the table, I couldn't help but notice that Atticus wasn't talking at all. He wasn't his normal self. He didn't even finish his pancakes.

After breakfast, me and Atticus did what we always do. We ran out the back door and headed out into the world.

I jumped off the back porch and rang the big black bell outside the farmhouse door. That's what we always did first. It's loud and you can hear it anywhere on the farm. Granny uses it to get Pop-pop's attention when he's out on the farm and forgets to turn on his cell phone. But today, Atticus didn't ring the bell with me.

We started down the big hilly pasture that leads to the barn. I tried not to step on any anthills or cow patties along the way. Atticus was so quiet. I cleared my throat hoping he might get the hint and tell me what was wrong.

"What?" he finally said.

"Oh, nothing," I said back.

"Okay," he said.

Finally, I couldn't take it. "What's the matter?"

"Nothing." He picked up a stick and threw it down the hill.

"I know you, Atticus Brightwell! So I know something's wrong!"

He didn't say anything.

"Atticus!"

"I got a B on my math test and my mom was all mad about it," he said. "That's all."

I looked at him funny. If he made a C, yes, Mrs. Brightwell would blow her top. But a B? Even she would probably let that one slide.

"You sure that's all it is?" I said, and looked at him harder.

"Yeah, I'm sure," he said, but he didn't look at me. That's when I knew Atticus was lying. I had only ever seen Atticus lie to one person before and that was his mother—and only when she left him no other choice.

Atticus had never lied to me.

"Come on, Charlie!" he suddenly yelled. Charlie, the chocolate Lab farm dog, started running toward us from the barn. Charlie weighs about as much as both of us put together and he likes to knock us down.

Atticus started running down the hill, his arms stretched out like wings on a plane. "Charlie," he yelled again, making the dog run faster.

"Stop, Atticus!" I yelled. For all of his smarts, Atticus is sometimes not so smart about animals.

I saw it coming. Then I saw them both go down. When I caught up with them, Charlie was on top of Atticus licking his face, and Atticus was laughing. It was the happiest Atticus had looked all day.

While I watched the two of them wrestling and playing, I made a decision—one that Atticus would have been proud of me for making if he had known about it. I decided not to ask him why he lied to me. I didn't want to force it out of him when he had clearly been so upset all morning. It wasn't like us to have secrets from each other but I knew in my heart that Atticus would tell me when he was ready.

After that, it was like things were normal again. We did all the usual things we do on the farm. We fed the trout in the pond. We walked along the big creek to the waterfall. We played pirates and made swords out of big sticks we found on the trail. And we visited Frank. Frank was no longer a little calf. He was a big bull and he was not going to end up a hamburger. Atticus had seen to that. He had made Pop-pop promise not to ever sell him.

Frank usually lived in the front pasture down the hill from Granny and Pop-pop's house. We were allowed to see him through the fence only. Atticus thinks that he can go inside and play with Frank like he used to, but I always remind him that that is a very bad idea. As Pop-pop has told us a hundred times, bulls can be unpredictable.

By the afternoon, Pop-pop found us. He drove up in his pickup truck and handed us a couple of little brown bags.

"Lunch," he said. "L-U-N-C-H." He winked at me. Sometimes I wish I never told him about me being a speller.

We headed for the big shed next to the barn and took our lunch into the hay house. Atticus always has his birthday party at the farm. The hay house was a big surprise that Pop-pop built for his sixth birthday. It takes up most of the shed and is made of all these hay bales stacked together with all kinds of tunnels and secret hiding places. You can climb through it, on top of it, and all around it. It's where we always eat lunch. It's the best place ever.

We settled into our favorite nook under all the hay with our peanut butter and jelly sandwiches. We broke off pieces for Charlie and watched him try to lap the peanut butter off the roof of his mouth.

Atticus reached in his pocket and pulled out an acorn and gave it to me. Acorns bring good luck.

"When did you find it?" I asked.

"Earlier," he replied, "when I went off to pee."

"Gross," I said, but took it anyway. I held up the acorn and looked at it. Imagine, a humongous oak tree coming from a little thing like that.

We sat across from each other leaning back on hay bales.

"Avie?"

"Yeah," I said.

"When do you think we're going to get our magical powers?"

"I don't know," I said. "When do you think we'll get them?"

"Well . . ." Atticus looked up and put on his thinking face. "It's been over four months since we turned ten—"

"Since you turned ten," I corrected. "Less than four months for me."

"I just thought something would have happened by now. That we'd at least have an idea of what they were going to be." He looked at me suddenly. "It hasn't happened to you yet, has it?"

"Unless my power has to do with sitting in Jell-O or spilling milk, then, no, it hasn't happened to me yet."

"You'll tell me, though? Right?"

"Yes, doofus," I said, smiling. Like I'd hide something like that from him. And then I realized I had been hiding something from him. Just like he had been hiding something from me earlier that day. "Atticus," I said, a little guiltily. "I haven't told you everything, though."

His eyes got wide. "What do you mean? What's happened?"

"Nothing, I promise. But . . . it's just this feeling I have. You know, sometimes late at night, I think I can feel my power." I pointed toward my stomach. "You know, deep in here. Can you?"

Atticus looked up. I could tell he was thinking. Finally, he said, "Yeah, I think I know what you mean. Like it's in there somewhere but not ready to come out yet."

"Exactly!" I exclaimed. Because that's exactly what it felt like. "I'm so glad you're feeling it, too."

Atticus smiled and I exhaled. It was good to share this with him. "I've been thinking about it a lot, though," I said. "I wonder what kind of powers we're going to get. I don't really care about running fast or anything like that. I want it to be something truly magical, Atticus."

"Like what?" he asked.

"I don't know yet." Sure, I wanted my Infinity power to help me with Elena or help me with my spelling, but I had a feeling it was supposed to be something more than that.

"Avie?"

"Yes, Atticus."

"I hope mine is flying."

By 7:30, we had been playing hearts with Caroline and Granny for about an hour when the phone rang. Mr. and Mrs. Brightwell were going to be late. Something about a carburetor.

I heard Pop-pop on the phone saying we could just stay the night but I could tell from his tone that that wasn't going to happen.

Granny put down her cards and said she would make us some dinner. "Add up the points to see who won," she said, and grinned. She already knew who won. Granny almost always wins at cards.

After dinner, I called my mom to let her know what was happening. She had just gotten home from the hospital. "Do I have to come get you, Avalon?" she asked. I heard her softly sighing.

"No. Mr. and Mrs. Brightwell are coming," I said. "But it might be awhile."

"Okay," she said. "Just try not to be too late."

I couldn't see how I would actually have any control over that—me being ten and not the one with the driver's license—but I said I would try and hung up the phone.

It was after 9:30 by the time Mr. and Mrs. Brightwell drove up. I don't see Mr. Brightwell much on account of he works for the government and travels a lot to foreign countries. Atticus is not sure exactly what he does so I have decided that must mean he is a government secret agent. A spy. And tonight, the spy was in a bad mood.

On the drive home, I wondered why we didn't just spend the night at the farm. I could tell that Mr. Brightwell thought that would have been a lot easier, too. I looked at Mrs. Brightwell from the backseat. She looked tired. It must be a lot of work being her.

Then I looked at Atticus. We had had a good day. I had almost forgotten that he had lied to me.

My mom was watching TV when I got home. M and I sat with her and watched the end of some old movie she had on. About these men who dressed up like women to be in this old-timey jazz band that you could only belong to if you were a girl. It was in black-and-white and it was weird but Mom seemed to like it.

When it finished, I asked if we could have a night-night snack before bed.

"Avalon, it's late," she said.

"Come on, Mom," I said, clapping M's paws together. "We're hungry."

She got up off the couch saying, "You know, you're at the age when you could make your own night-night snack."

I frowned. She used to like making me snacks.

As she walked to the kitchen, I noticed the pile of mail on the counter. I slipped M off my lap and made my way toward the stack. Bill . . . bill . . . something from the hospital . . . another bill—

"There's no letter, Avalon," she said.

I pretended like I didn't care. "I was just looking."

"You need to stop looking," she said, and dished me out a scoop of ice cream. She put the bowl on the counter in front of me and handed me a spoon. "I'm serious."

"I know," I said quietly. I did know. And I knew she was right, too. Why should I keep looking? Hadn't the last year taught me anything? I hadn't gotten any mail for a long time. Why should today be different?

I took the spoon from Mom and started eating. I usually loved rocky road, but tonight it didn't taste so good. I silently wished that my Infinity Year power would magically bring me the letter I was hoping for.

Afterward, while I was brushing my teeth, Mom said good night, then M and I went to our room.

As I got undressed, I pulled the acorn Atticus gave me out of my pocket and put it on my bedside table. For luck. I crawled into bed and M curled up beside me. It was late and everything was quiet. I thought about my Infinity Year power and after a minute, I felt it. Just like those other times. Deep down inside, quiet and not yet reachable, but in there all right. Like it still wasn't ready to show itself but wanted me to know that it was there, waiting for the time to be right. It made me happy that Atticus was feeling it, too.

M and I fell asleep and dreamed we were sleeping under a humongous oak tree. It was the biggest tree I had ever seen and it stood alone in an infinite sea of grass. A wind began to blow and it made the grass rise and fall like waves. Atticus was there and he was trying to tell me something. But I couldn't hear him. The wind was too loud.

FIVE

A great thing happened today. Mrs. Jackson told me to stay behind when the rest of the class was going to lunch. At first, I thought this was the opposite of great. Like she had noticed me chewing gum at recess or accidentally-on-purpose taking all the tops off Elena's Magic Markers and she was going to tell me off for it.

Instead, she had noticed that I'm a fantastic speller. F-A-N-T-A-S-T-I-C. Fantastic.

She pulled out all of my spelling quizzes and showed me how I had never gotten a word wrong. Then she looked me right in the eye and said, "Our classroom spelling bee is in two weeks. You should win it pretty easily. So, I'm thinking we should start getting you ready for the school bee in January."

I must have looked pretty dumbfounded, because my mouth just hung open and I couldn't say a thing.

"Are you all right, Avalon?" she asked.

All right? I was doing somersaults inside. The school bee! In January! Hooray!

I had a profound realization. Everyone had been wrong about Mrs. Jackson. She was not the worst teacher in the fifth grade. She was the greatest teacher there had ever been in the entire history of the world.

"You really think I can win?" I finally asked.

"Here in the class, yes. I don't think you have a chance to win the school bee. Harinder Singh is a formidable speller. I expect he will win again this year. But the second-place finalist will go with him to the regional bee in April." She smiled and all her wrinkles crinkled up. "I think you have a chance at that."

Hari Singh. The regional bee. It was like a dream coming true. Could it be possible that my Infinity Year power was about spelling after all?

"And you're just in fifth grade, Avalon. In a couple of years, you might be as good a speller as he."

I smiled. I was starting my professional life as a speller. And Mrs. Jackson was going to help.

She gave me a hall pass to go to the lunchroom by myself. I walked through the hall feeling completely happy and free. I couldn't help but think of my dad.

My dad is the reason I can spell like I do. He used to say

that I came by it honestly, that I was a *chip off the old block*. We used to play spelling games and he was so proud when I got words like *shambolic* and *pomegranate* right.

Right now, my dad is neither happy nor free. He's the third reason I'm somewhat famous at my school. Because my dad is in prison. Has been for nearly a year. That's why he's never around. That's why I never talk about him. That's why last year was the worst year of my life.

Dad worked at the car dealership in town. He was the manager there and I used to go down on Saturday afternoons and hang out with him in his office and watch all the excitement of people coming in to buy cars. When it was really busy, I'd go help Vidal and Roberto in the detail department. I'd clean the inside windows of the just-sold cars so they wouldn't have to.

It was fun being there. My dad was important and everybody was nice to me.

Nobody knew that my dad was stealing.

My mom never told me all the details, but I read about it in the local paper. Something about cars being sold to people they shouldn't have sold them to. My dad and two of his salesmen went to prison last fall.

My dad wasn't a thief. At least, I didn't think so. Some days I wake up, and for a second, I don't remember what's happened. Then it all rushes back. My dad would have grounded me for stealing so much as a pack of gum. He would have made me take it back and apologize in person. That's just the kind of guy he was. I thought. But it turns out, he wasn't. How could he have done this?

The year before had been so different. My dad had been really happy. The dealership was selling more cars than ever, and it was all because of him. My dad was making plans. He wanted to buy us a bigger house. He wanted to take me to see the ocean.

Then he went to the owner, Mrs. Prescott, and asked for a raise. After that, he didn't seem very happy anymore. I remember thinking how he seemed kind of mad all the time.

During the trial, I went to live with my Grandma Grace in Tennessee. My mom said it would be better for me.

It was *so* not better for me. I didn't know anyone there. School was a nightmare and I really missed Atticus.

I was gone for sixty-one days. I counted each of them off on my Cats of the World calendar. I missed two very important things:

1. Seeing my dad before he went off to state prison for the next four years.
2. The fourth-grade classroom spelling bee.

We haven't visited my dad once in prison, so that means it's over a year since I've seen him. I've spoken to him on the phone two times. He called last Christmas and on my mother's birthday. Mom gave me the phone both times. She had stopped talking to him before I was shipped off to

Tennessee, before the trial. On the phone with him, I tried to sound like everything was normal but it wasn't. He didn't sound like himself. And I guess I didn't sound like me, either.

During the whole time, he's sent me only four letters. The first one was pretty long and told me how he would beat this thing and come home soon. The second one was shorter and talked about how the prison food was so bad. The third one, well, the third one just sounded sad. He wrote that he wanted me to come visit but by the end of the letter said it was probably a bad idea. The last letter wasn't really a letter but a birthday card with a stupid store-bought message inside. At the bottom of the card he wrote only four words—*Love you kid, Dad.*

I send him a letter every week. I think he must feel bad, so I hope my letters cheer him up. I get the stamps from Mrs. White and I always mail the letters from the mailbox at the top of our street. My mom doesn't know I'm writing him. Mom is still really mad at my dad. If she found out I was writing him, I bet she'd be really mad at me, too.

The only person I ever talk to about this is Atticus. He never asks me about it, though. He knows it's something I don't want to talk about unless I want to talk about it.

The thing about the school spelling bee is this: The spellers invite their families to come and watch. They sit in the audience and cheer. My dad would have loved to see me up there. He would have yelled louder than anyone.

But since he's not here and my mom will probably have to work, there won't be much of a cheering section for me.

That's the thing.

At lunch, I told Atticus what Mrs. Jackson said about my spelling and how she thought I might have a chance to make it to the regional bee.

"That's awesome," he said, leaning over from his table. "Can I have a french fry?"

I passed my tray to him at the Ms. Smith table so Atticus could grab some fries. His mom didn't let him buy lunch on french fry days.

"Me and M will help you study," he said through a mouthful of potatoes.

I laughed. Atticus and M were about as good as each other at spelling. It was the one thing that I could do way better than him.

"We need to talk about our magical powers, too," he whispered, leaning between the tables so nobody else could hear. "Any news?"

"Not yet," I said. Atticus asked me about this daily. It was always on his mind. I wondered what he would do if I got mine first. It might drive him crazy!

Across the room, I saw Hari Singh laughing with some of his friends at one of the seventh-grade tables. It would be cool if my Infinity Year power made me a great speller like him. Or it would be great if it saved me from Elena's evil plans. But deep down inside, I really wanted one thing. Even though he had done something really bad, I wanted my Infinity power for my father. I wanted him to write me a letter. Or give me a call. I wanted my mom not to be mad at him anymore. I wanted us to be a family again.

In the afternoon, our classroom went to the art room to work on our Family Tree Project. Mae and I sat on the floor in one corner of the room with all of our supplies around us. We had to make three posters. One about my family, one about her family, and one about things both our families had in common. We had to include diagrams and drawings and pictures. The diagrams were supposed to trace back all the way to our great-great-grandparents.

Mae is very good at drawing and I am very good at gluing so we are perfectly matched. We had to make our presentation to the class right before Thanksgiving.

So far, we had been doing research trying to figure out who all our relatives were. We'd just started making copies of the pictures we'd found and began gluing them on our poster board.

The week before, I called Grandma Grace, who told me all kinds of things on the phone. Like how her father fought in World War II and how her great-grandmother marched in parades to get women the vote. Grandma Grace is good at stories and history. She is the editor in chief of her town's weekly newspaper in Tennessee called the *Sanford Telegraph*. She sent me all kinds of pictures she copied from my mother's side of the family.

"Who is that again?" Mae asked, pointing at one of my black-and-white pictures.

"I think that's my great-great-grandfather," I said, and turned over the photo. Grandma Grace had written everyone's name and how they related to me on the back of each picture. Thank goodness. And this was, in fact, Great-great-granddad. "His name was Talmadge Guest," I said, and held up the photo so Mae could see it better. "Do we know any Talmadges?"

"I don't think so," Mae said, and smiled. As she searched through her photos, I looked at Talmadge Guest again. His thin lips drew a straight line across his wrinkled face. Obviously never heard of sunscreen. Maybe never heard of a smile. If he lived in this century, I thought he'd be at home with the phrase *Hey kid, get off my lawn.*

"Look at this one." Mae held up one of her black-and-white photos of a man who looked even scarier than Talmadge Guest. He had a long gray beard and round glasses that sat on the end of his nose.

"Yikes!" I said. "Who's he?"

She looked down at her notebook to double-check his name. "This is Adam Wasserman. He came from Poland in . . . 1904." She read from the notes she had made with her mom. "He and his wife, Freda, landed at Ellis Island and started a new life in Brooklyn, New York."

I looked at Adam Wasserman more closely. He had even more wrinkles than Talmadge Guest did. It must have been even harder to live in Poland than in Tennessee.

"These are my great-grandparents from my mother's side of the family," Mae said, showing me another old picture. The man and woman in this photo were old like the other ones. They both had gray hair and glasses. But these ancestors looked nice. They had kind faces. They were even smiling. "Mom says they could have been killed. It was a miracle that they survived. Mom says if they hadn't escaped, we never would have existed."

"What do you mean?" I asked.

"Well, we're Jewish, and they lived in Nazi Germany. That was before World War II," she said as she studied the photo. "They had to sneak out of their house in the middle of the night with just a couple of suitcases and some forged passports. Mom said it took them three months to make it all the way to America."

Wow. We had studied Nazi Germany in class this year. About how Jewish people were killed by the Nazis in concentration camps. When we learned about it, it seemed really bad but somehow, being part of history, it also seemed kind of distant. Now, hearing a story like this directly from Mae's lips, it seemed not only really bad but really *real*.

"Did your mom know them?" I asked.

"She said she met them when she was little but doesn't remember them much. Just knows about them through stories." She arranged the photo on one of the poster boards and then looked over at what I was working on.

"Do you have any old pictures from your dad's family tree?" she asked.

"Not yet," I said quietly.

I'd got everything I needed about my mom's family, but my dad's family was a problem. I wrote him to ask about his ancestors but he hasn't written back. His parents live way out in California and we don't talk to them much, especially now. So, I don't know what to do. Maybe I'll make up names and stick them to old pictures I find on the Internet. An imaginary family. One with a dad who didn't go to—

"That's going to be embarrassing to explain." The voice came from above. I looked up and saw Elena staring down at my poster board. She was pointing right at the spot where my father's picture would be.

"Maybe everybody doesn't know about your dad," she said. "Does Mae even know?"

She looked at Mae. I was sure Mae knew my dad was in prison. Everybody knew. We just hadn't talked about it yet.

Mae didn't say anything, and I couldn't take my eyes off Elena's face. After my dad went to prison, Elena had been extra mean to me. She even took a picture of my dad from the newspaper and drew prison bars across his face and posted it on the fourth-grade bulletin board. That had been the last straw. The next week I took that picture of her and her American flag underwear.

"If I were Mae, I'd be embarrassed to even be your partner," Elena snarled.

I looked down. "Shut up, Elena," I said quietly. Mae still didn't say a word. Maybe she was embarrassed to be working with me. Maybe Elena was right.

"I wouldn't blame her one bit," Elena taunted.

It's bad enough when Elena says things about me. When she says stuff about my family, it's worse. I felt my face start to burn. I wanted to jump up and push her away. This was a moment when I really wished for Atticus. He'd know how to stop me. But he wasn't there.

I dropped my marker and began to rise, like one of the erupting volcanoes at the back of Ms. Smith's class. I suddenly didn't care about anything Elena had planned for me. I was ready to end this thing now.

"Elena!" Mrs. Jackson suddenly called out from across the room. "Back to your work, please," she said. Elena narrowed her eyes at me before turning to go. As she walked away, I saw Mrs. Jackson looking at me. She gave me a little smile before she went back to helping Eva Chang and Marcus with their project.

In that moment, I realized if Mrs. Jackson caught Elena in the act, she would be on my side. Maybe I should tell her what I had heard in the bathroom at the open house. Maybe. But if I did, I knew Elena would just deny it. She would say I was the liar and then nothing would change.

I sat back down across from Mae and tried to act normal. We went back to organizing our photos like nothing happened.

By the time Atticus's class got to recess, I was ready to boil over. He could tell something was wrong right away. We walked past the jungle gym and sat down on the swings.

I told him what happened and how mad I was at Elena.

"Don't listen to her," he said.

"But why does she do it, Atticus?"

He shrugged. "I know she started it but . . ."

I was glad he didn't finish that sentence, but I knew what he meant. Elena might have started it but I never seemed to let it end.

"I don't know," he said. "Maybe she got dropped on her head when she was a baby."

"And Mae didn't say anything. Even afterward," I said. "Do you think she doesn't know about my dad?"

Atticus raised his eyebrow at me.

"Okay, she knows about him," I said. "Of course she knows."

"Yeah," he said.

I dug my toe into the worn ground beneath the swing. "Atticus," I said, and looked around to be sure nobody was listening. "I know you want a big Infinity Year power but really, I only want one thing."

He looked over at me.

"I just want my dad to write me back," I said. Tears welled up in my eyes and I quickly brushed them away.

"He'll write," Atticus said. "Your dad's not a bad guy."

I tried to smile. Of course, that's what Atticus would think. He always thinks the best of everybody. My mom says that Atticus is guileless. I looked it up one time in the dictionary. It means someone who is innocent and naive. I don't know if that's true about Atticus but I have never heard him say a bad word about anyone.

Not about my dad.

Not even about Jasper Hightower.

That's how we became best friends. It was first grade, and it changed the course of Avalon history. I knew Atticus. Everyone knew Atticus. His sister, Caroline, was the Queen of Eighth Grade, and his family lived up on Bunker Hill.

Jasper Hightower used to live down the street from me. He was the kind of boy who would set an ant on fire with a magnifying glass and laugh. My mom would walk me to school every day while Jasper walked with his older brothers.

I'd overhear things. Like how they were going to toilet paper somebody's yard or how they were going to steal somebody's lunch money or dunk somebody's head in a toilet. I remember feeling sorry for Jasper because I knew his brothers were bad. And that didn't leave much room for Jasper to be good.

I kept my distance until one day I heard them talking about Atticus. Jasper's brothers hated the kids who lived up on Bunker Hill. They hated their nice houses and their nice lives. They decided that, for the fun of it, Jasper should play a trick on Atticus.

Atticus had seemed like a nice guy to me. So what if he lived on Bunker Hill? So what if his sister was the Queen of Eighth Grade?

One afternoon during recess, I was at the very top of the jungle gym. From my perch, I saw Atticus following Jasper back inside the school. That was weird. We weren't supposed to do that.

So, I decided to follow them.

I jumped down and hurried inside just in time to see them going into the boys' room at the end of the hall. Nobody saw this but me.

I was only in first grade. I didn't have a hall pass. I knew I'd get in trouble if anybody caught me. But I couldn't get the vision of Atticus getting his head dunked in the toilet out of my mind. So, like the six-year-old superhero that I was, I busted into the boys' bathroom.

Whatever was about to happen hadn't happened yet. But I could tell it was about to. I started jabbering on about how Mrs. Warneke was looking for them and she was really mad. That even got Jasper scared. Jasper suddenly ran out of the bathroom, leaving me and Atticus in there alone.

Atticus looked confused but glad to see me. "Thanks," he said.

"You're welcome," I said back.

We've had each other's backs ever since.

Later I learned that Jasper had told Atticus that someone had left him a prize in the middle stall. I still can't believe he fell for that one.

Luckily for Atticus, Jasper and his brothers moved away the very next year.

I wish I'd been so lucky with Elena.

SIX

In our school, the classroom spelling bees are on the second Friday in October. I made over five hundred flashcards and had been studying harder than ever.

Ever since Mrs. Jackson noticed I was a fantastic speller, we had been doing spelling drills together every Monday and Wednesday afternoon.

During our drills, I would sit across from Mrs. Jackson's desk and we would start practicing. She'd ask me word after word and it was my job to spell them. The week before the classroom bee, I spelled every one of them correctly except *pseudonym*.

How was I supposed to know that the *p* was silent? I spelled it S-E-U-D-O-N-Y-M—which made complete sense to me because the word doesn't start with a *p* sound, it starts with an *s* sound.

"A *pseudonym* is a fictitious name, esp. one assumed by an author." That's what it says in the dictionary. *Esp.* is short for *especially*.

Mrs. Jackson had been teaching me about word origins and how they can help me figure out how to spell things. For instance, *pseudonym* comes from the Greek words *pseudo* (which means "false") and *nym* (which means "name"). Put them together and you get *false name*. Also, she taught me that if a word has a Greek origin and begins with an *s* sound, it probably starts with a *p*.

Probably. But not always. That made my head hurt a little. There are so many rules to learn. I'm not so sure about these silent-letter words.

Mrs. Jackson taught me how a spelling bee works and said that unlike some of the other classrooms, we would be strictly adhering to the official rules during our classroom bee. Every class in the school (grades four through eight) had a bee on the very same day. The top two winners from each class would then advance to the school-wide spelling bee in January.

Atticus came over on the Sunday before the bee to help me study. While he quizzed me on words at the kitchen table, my mom sat at the counter, letting out the hem on my favorite pair of red pants.

"Systematic," Atticus said, reading off one of my flash-cards.

"S-Y-S-T-E-M-A-T-I-C," I spelled.

"Right," Atticus said. He put that flashcard on the bottom of the pile and picked another one. "Consternation."

"C-O-N-S-T-E-R-N-A-T-I-O-N."

"Correct," he said. "Kevin and Adam are definitely going as Iron Man and Ant-Man," he continued. "I think I want to be Captain America."

We had been trying to figure out our Halloween costumes for the past two weeks but nothing seemed right yet. As a rule, we liked to go as a pair.

My mom looked up from her sewing. "You'd be a perfect Captain America, Atticus."

He smiled at her and picked up another flashcard.

"Then what am I supposed to be?" I asked as M jumped onto the kitchen table.

"You can be the Wasp," he said enthusiastically. "Or the Black Widow."

"Maybe—" I started to say, but Mom cut me off.

"Not the Black Widow," she said. "She's too . . . grown-up."

"Then who?" I asked. "There aren't any other girl Avengers." I looked at Atticus, who was frowning at the flashcard in his hand. He was actually a lot like Captain America. Reliable (always). Honest (mostly). Indefatigable (look it up). And then Captain America got up from the table and helplessly showed the flashcard to my mom. Spelling challenged (without a doubt).

"*Obsidian*," she told Atticus. "It means 'black,' like the Widow."

"Cool," Atticus said. "The Obsidian Widow."

I looked at my mom. "Could I be her if we called me that?"

"Nice try," she said, and turned back to her sewing. "You'll come up with something."

By the time we finished all the words, we still hadn't come up with something and it was time for Atticus to go home.

The following week, we talked about Halloween every day at recess but mostly I was thinking about my spelling words. Atticus finally gave up and said we would talk about it after the bee because I wasn't giving our costumes the serious thought they deserved.

He wasn't mad or anything. He was right. My mind was cluttered full of words and letters. I just couldn't make any more room for Halloween.

The night before the classroom bee, I sat up with M until almost one o'clock in the morning. I couldn't sleep. Words kept running through my head, and every few minutes, I would look one up just to be sure I was spelling it right.

The morning of the bee, M sat on the toilet seat and watched me read off the flashcards that were taped onto the bathroom mirror. I brushed my teeth and looked at them over and over again.

"You're going to brush your teeth off," my mom said as she stopped at the bathroom door. "Don't you think you're ready?"

I just looked at her.

"Of course you're ready!" she said, and kissed me on the side of my forehead.

I spit out the toothpaste and wiped my mouth. I guess I was as ready as I would ever be.

Mrs. Jackson's classroom bee began at 10:00 a.m. on Friday, October 13. You heard me. Friday the thirteenth! For someone as superstitious as me, this was alarming. One of the biggest days of my life was falling on the unluckiest day of the year. It could only be worse if I had to stand on a sidewalk crack while I was spelling. I did what I could: I crossed my fingers all the way to school; I carried Atticus's acorn in my pocket; I walked around Mr. Dale's ladder. But would it be enough? Maybe I would need my Infinity Year magic for spelling after all!

The first round began. In alphabetical order, Mrs. Jackson called each of us to the podium in the front of the room. Mae went first. Mrs. Jackson asked her to spell *microscope*. She spelled it right, I am pleased to report, and then sat down again. Eva Chang was next. She got the word *enormous*. Eva spelled it E-N-O-R-M-U-S. Mrs. Jackson rang a little bell on her desk letting us know that Eva had gotten the word wrong. Eva slapped her hand to her forehead and sat back down in her seat. Mrs. Jackson then spelled *enormous* correctly for us.

By the time it was my turn, three of my classmates had already been eliminated. When Mrs. Jackson called my name, I walked to the podium.

"Avalon," she said. "Please spell the word *handsome*."

Even though this was an easy word and I could spell it in my sleep, I am a trained professional and I am allowed to ask certain questions. So I did.

"Could you repeat the word, please?" I asked.

"Handsome," she said.

"Could you please use the word in a sentence?"

"Yes," Mrs. Jackson said. "The handsome man walked down the street and stopped three times to look at his reflection in the department store's window. Handsome."

It was a good sentence.

Then I asked, "The definition, please?"

Mrs. Jackson smiled a little. She knew I didn't need the definition. "Handsome," she repeated. "A fine form or figure. Good-looking. Or generous, as in a handsome present. Handsome."

"What's the word's origin?" I asked. I heard Elena groan.

"Old English. Before that it relates to the Germanic. Handsome."

It was great. We were doing it just like we did in the drills.

"Handsome," I said. "H-A-N-D-S-O-M-E," I spelled. "Handsome," I said again.

I waited for a moment. No bell rang. "Correct," Mrs. Jackson said. "You may take your seat, Avalon."

I sat down happily. I had spelled my first word in my very first spelling bee.

Each round the words got more difficult. Mrs. Jackson rang the bell twelve times during the third round. By the fourth round, there were only three of us left. There was me, Isabel Fernandez, and Elena Maxwell. Isabel Fernandez is one of those quiet girls who wears glasses and reads a lot. I knew she would be trouble. And then there was Elena. She would just love out-spelling me. I could not let that happen.

Isabel went up first. She got the word *tributary* and spelled it correctly. Next, it was my turn. I got the word *odyssey*. I found myself looking at Elena. She squinted her eyes and gave me such a horrible look. I wanted to beat her so bad.

I asked Mrs. Jackson about the word. I asked her the part of speech. I asked her to use the word in a sentence. She told me *odyssey* comes from the Greek meaning "voyage" or "journey." But I wasn't listening. I was thinking about Elena.

Ever since the bathroom incident, I had felt myself getting more and more nervous. It had been almost two months since I overheard Elena plotting my demise, but it still hadn't happened. Whatever she was planning had to be coming soon. I was starting to expect it at almost every moment.

Mrs. Jackson cleared her throat. I knew that was her way of telling me to hurry up and answer.

"Odyssey," I finally said. "O-D-Y-S-E-Y," I spelled. "Odyssey," I said again.

There was a painful moment when I realized I had not spelled the word out in my head before I spelled it out loud. I had violated a major rule of spelling.

The bell on Mrs. Jackson's desk rang. Friday the thirteenth had struck and it had struck hard.

My odyssey was over.

I sat down at my desk and put my head down on my arms. I knew that word. I knew it had two *S*s. What had I been thinking?

I felt Elena brush past me as she walked to the podium. She was going to be insufferable from now on. I-N-S-U-F-F-E-R-A-B-L-E. I didn't think I could stand it. I had worked so hard, and I let one dirty look from her ruin it all.

Note to self: Infinity Year power DOES NOT help with spelling.

I heard Mrs. Jackson give Elena her word. *Congenial.* How easy. HOW EASY! I listened as she spelled it:

"C-O-N-G-E-N-E-A-L," she spelled. "Congenial," she then said.

My head popped up off my desk. Just as the bell rang.

"I'm sorry, Elena, but that's incorrect," Mrs. Jackson said. "*Congenial* is spelled C-O-N-G-E-N-I-A-L. Please return to your seat."

Elena walked past me in a real huff and accidentally-on-purpose knocked a book off Marcus's desk.

"This leads to a very interesting situation, class," Mrs. Jackson said as she stood up from her desk. "First, we must congratulate Isabel Fernandez—the winner of our classroom spelling bee. Let's give her a round of applause."

Everybody clapped and I could see Isabel's face turning red.

"Isabel will be representing our class in the school-wide spelling bee in January that will take place in the Grover Cleveland Lunchroom and Auditorium." She looked at Isabel and crinkled her eyes. "And I know you will represent us proudly, Isabel.

"However," she continued. "We must send one more representative." She looked at me and Elena. "This is how this is going to work. Avalon and Elena will continue spelling. The one who goes the longest without getting a word wrong will win. Avalon, you're first."

I took a deep breath. Then I stood up and walked to the podium.

Over the next eight rounds, these were the words we got:

	MY WORDS	HER WORDS
Round 1	hyperbole	population
Round 2	ounce	finalist
Round 3	behoove	barley
Round 4	tremulous	continent
Round 5	missile	whirlpool
Round 6	newfangled	colonization
Round 7	worrisome	outrageous
Round 8	pinafore	mermaid

We both spelled them all correctly. I couldn't help but think that my words were a little harder than hers, but I knew that couldn't really be true.

Until I got my ninth-round word.

Psoriasis.

I did not know this word. It had not been on any of my flashcards and I had never seen it on any of my spelling lists.

I didn't mean to but I looked at Elena for just a second. She had a little mean smile on her face. I could tell she knew I had no idea how to spell my word.

I looked down and closed my eyes. *Psoriasis.*

"Could you please repeat the word?" I asked.

Mrs. Jackson did.

"Could you please use the word in a sentence?"

She did that, too. I listened hard but I still didn't know how to spell it.

I started thinking about how it sounded and tried to look at it inside my head. S-O-R-I-A-S-I-S. Yeah, that looked right. That could be right. At least, it was the best guess I could come up with.

"Could you please tell me the word's origin?" I asked.

"Yes, it comes from the Greek. *Psoriasis*," she said.

I started to smile. It came from the Greek. Those wonderful Greeks and their silent *P*s.

"Psoriasis," I said. "P-S-O-R-I-A-S-I-S," I spelled. "Psoriasis," I said again.

I waited and looked at Mrs. Jackson.

"Correct," she said, and I let out the biggest sigh ever.

Elena and I passed each other as I went back to my desk. Marcus patted me on my shoulder as I sat down. I looked up at Elena at the podium.

"*Nightingale*," Mrs. Jackson said.

"Could you repeat it?" Elena asked.

"Nightingale."

"Could you give me the definition?" she asked.

"Nightingale. A small reddish-brown migratory thrush. The male of the bird species sings powerfully and melodically in the day and night. Nightingale."

"What is the word's origin?" she asked. Elena had been paying attention.

"Old English," Mrs. Jackson responded.

This time I caught Elena looking at me. I fought the impulse to stick out my tongue at her. I wanted to win this fair and square so I stayed completely still, my tongue staying firmly inside my mouth.

"Nightingale," she said. "N-I-G-H-T-I-N-G-A-I-L," she spelled. "Nightingale."

There was a long moment of silence in Mrs. Jackson's fifth-grade class. Then the little bell rang.

Everybody looked at me and started clapping. I had won. Well, I had really come in second, but I had beaten Elena and that was a win for me.

As Elena stomped back to her desk, Mrs. Jackson called me and Isabel up to the front of the class.

"First of all, I want to say, good job, Elena," Mrs. Jackson said. "You did extremely well today and should be very proud." Elena smiled at Mrs. Jackson and then she glared at me.

I didn't care. Because what Mrs. Jackson said next made everything else okay. "Let's all congratulate Isabel and Avalon, who will be representing our class in the Grover Cleveland School-Wide Spelling Bee!"

Everybody clapped and yelled. Isabel and I smiled at each other.

It was probably the best morning of my life.

By the time I told Atticus what happened at lunchtime, I was completely out of breath.

"Don't you want to know how I did?" he asked after I finished.

"Yes," I said excitedly. It would be so great if we were both in the big bee.

"I made it all the way to the second round," he said, and grinned.

I laughed. "Congratulations. I'm so proud."

After Atticus left to join his class line at the end of lunch, I felt a humongous smile growing inside. I looked up at the stage in the Grover Cleveland Lunchroom and Auditorium and pictured myself there. The big school-wide spelling bee was in January and January wasn't that far away.

There was a tap on my shoulder and I turned around. Hari Singh was looking down at me. "Hey, little speller," he said.

"Hi," I answered. "I'm Avalon."

"I know, dork," he said. "Don't you think I'd remember you?"

Oh, yeah. How could he forget me? Last time we talked, I was wearing a carton of milk.

"I wanted to congratulate you," he said, and sat down beside me. "Mrs. Jackson said you did really well today."

"Did she tell you I missed a word and came in second?"

"Yeah, who cares about that. Just nerves. You'll get used to it. Main thing is Mrs. Jackson has taken you under her wing. She doesn't do that with everyone. You must be pretty talented."

I blushed. I couldn't help it. "How do you know all this?" I asked.

· "Talent knows talent," he said, and grinned. "I used to be in Mrs. Jackson's class, too."

Wow. I could picture it. Hari Singh doing spelling drills across the desk from Mrs. Jackson in the very seat that I sat in every Monday and Wednesday afternoon.

He looked up at the stage. "Just remember, it's all about you and the words. Don't let anybody else get in your head."

I nodded. He was right.

"Did you win today?" I asked.

He opened his hands and shrugged. "What do you think?"

We both laughed. Of course he won. Nobody in this school could out-spell Hari Singh. And, by the way, that's Singh with a silent *h*.

SEVEN

On Halloween morning, Darth Vader walked into our classroom.

Darth Vader was extremely tall and, beneath his black Darth Vader robe, he wore white Adidas tennis shoes. Our principal, Mr. Peterson, was also extremely tall and always wore white Adidas tennis shoes.

"Good morning, Mrs. Jackson's class," Darth Vader said through his Darth Vader helmet in that real Darth Vader voice.

"Hello, Mr. Peterson," everyone said back.

"I'm not Mr. Peterson," he said. "We have taken Mr. Peterson to the Death Star. I am the new principal. I, Darth Vader, am now your leader."

Marcus Johnson thought this was hilarious. He started

laughing and snorting behind me. I could sense the snot running down his nose.

"Mrs. Jackson," he continued, "please let your classroom know that we have arranged certain events around the noon hour that should bring chills and goose bumps to all fifth graders who dare to board our Imperial starship, located in what used to be the Grover Cleveland Lunchroom and Auditorium."

I hoped he hadn't talked to the kindergarten classes like this. Some of them might have wet their pants.

"I will do that, Mr. Pet—I mean Mr. Vader," Mrs. Jackson said. She was dressed like a cowgirl, with a cowboy hat and boots and a lasso draped over the back of her chair.

Before turning to go, Mr. Peterson took a step forward and stopped right in front of my desk. He looked down at me and said, "You should be especially afraid."

For a second, I got scared. What was he talking about? Then I remembered how I was dressed. I was Princess Leia, warrior princess, wearing a long white gown and a bun on each side of my head. And he was my evil father.

I grinned and he turned, whirling his cape. He stomped out of our classroom and headed for Ms. Smith's room.

Atticus was going to be so pleased. "Ah, my son!" I heard Darth Vader's voice bellow from next door. Mr. Peterson had clearly just seen his son (my Atticus), Luke Skywalker.

Everybody always dresses up for Halloween at my school. Everybody. It's just the thing to do at Grover C.

Even after the spelling bee was over and I had more room in my brain, Atticus and I hadn't been able to figure out who we were going to be until the weekend before Halloween. I was over at his house and we still couldn't agree on anything. So, we did what we usually did in such situations. We put on *Star Wars Episode IV.*

As soon as the hologram of Princess Leia came out of R2-D2, we knew it was right, at the exact same time. Plus, with everything going on with Elena, we thought it was a good idea to have the Force Be With Us this Halloween.

Mom had been making my costume from the material of an old dress she didn't wear anymore. I was scared it wasn't going to be finished in time, and when I woke up on Halloween morning, she was still working on it at the kitchen table.

"I'm almost done," she said when she saw me walk out my bedroom door, yawning. "Why are you up so early?"

I looked at my costume that was lying across the kitchen table. "I had a dream I was the only one in class who didn't have a Halloween costume," I said, wiping the sleep from my eyes.

"Well, that is a dream that will not be coming true." She made one last stitch and slipped the costume over my head. I put my arms through and Mom zipped up the back.

She stood there looking at me for the longest time.

"What's wrong?" I finally asked. "Do I look stupid?"

Mom smiled. I hadn't seen her smile like that for a long time. She grabbed my hand. "Come see."

We ran into her bedroom and stood together in front of her full-length mirror. We both just looked at me. I don't know what I was expecting. But it wasn't this.

I looked . . . good. Here I was, regular me, looking like a space warrior princess.

Suddenly, we both started to laugh. We couldn't help ourselves. It was pretty terrific.

The night before, I'd decided I was going to tell my mom about Elena and her plot against me. Halloween would be the perfect time for Elena to strike. But seeing my mom laughing that morning had changed my mind. I didn't want to ruin it.

Atticus and I had been on high alert for the past week though—ever since Adam had overheard Chloe talking to Samantha Cooper on the bus. He couldn't hear exactly what they were saying but it was something about Halloween and it was something about me.

The day before Halloween, me and Atticus were still trying to come up with a plan to stop Elena but nothing seemed good enough. At recess, we were sitting at the top of the jungle gym when we officially ran out of ideas.

"Maybe we don't need a plan," Atticus finally said.

I looked at him funny. "That's a great idea," I said. "Are you crazy? We really need a plan."

"No, listen, Avie. Have you ever thought that our magical powers are just waiting for something like this to be activated?"

"Activated?" I asked. "Did you just say activated?"

Atticus groaned. "Seriously," he said. "That's how all superheroes get their powers. When they need them most."

"We're not superheroes."

"Yeah, but this is our Infinity Year," he said, suddenly whispering. "If we're ever going to get a superpower, it's going to be now."

It all sounded grand. But something in the back of my head had been bothering me. It had been months since our Infinity Year began, and we were still the same Avalon and Atticus. I couldn't help but wonder . . .

What if Pop-pop was wrong?

By lunchtime on Halloween, nothing bad had happened. Mrs. Jackson's class walked single file into the Imperial starship (the Grover Cleveland Lunchroom and Auditorium) at 12:05.

There were planets all over the walls and distant stars on the ceiling. There were model starships on every table and the lunch ladies were dressed like stormtroopers.

Mae waited for me in the lunch line. She was dressed as Snow White and carried a bright red apple. Behind us, I saw three witches. Yes, Elena, Sissy, and Chloe were dressed as witches. Imagine that.

I carried my tray of mystery meat and french fries across the lunchroom and passed the seventh-grade tables. Vampire Hari Singh was sitting next to two zombies with blood on their faces and really dirty-looking hair. One of them had a hatchet coming out of his head. The other looked like he had lost a hand.

I sat down at the end of my table next to Luke Skywalker. It was really Atticus, sitting at the end of his table, as usual. Kevin had taken off his Iron Man mask so he could eat. Adam was wearing his cybernetic helmet and shoving french fries up his nose.

"Hello, Leia," Luke/Atticus said. "Any activity on the witch front, yet?"

"Nothing, Luke," I said. "But I can tell they're up to something."

Kevin banged his fist on their table. "We got your back, Avalon! That Elena better start watching hers."

"Yeah," said Adam as one of the french fries fell out of his nose. Kevin and Adam meant well but I knew they were both a little scared of Elena.

Darth Vader/Mr. Peterson walked through the lunchroom dramatically, his cape flowing behind him. The lights suddenly went out. There was a crack of thunder and somebody started turning the lights on and off so it would look like lightning.

Then the lights came back on and Darth Vader was gone. We waited for something else to happen but nothing did.

"*That* was the scary thing Mr. Peterson had planned?" Atticus said.

"Whoa," said Kevin. "That was super scary."

"Look! I've got goose bumps!" Adam said, and stuck out his arm so we could see the goose bumps that weren't really there.

We all laughed. I decided I shouldn't worry too much about the kindergartners being scared after all.

The rest of the day went by without anything unusual happening. Which was weird. The bell rang at 3:15 and I watched with growing relief as the witches left the classroom with the rest of the class.

After school, I waited with Atticus at his bus line. He said he could walk me home, but I knew his mother wouldn't like that because she would be getting ready for Halloween and would want him to help. We always trick-or-treated in Atticus's neighborhood on Bunker Hill because it was the best Halloween street in our town. All the houses got really decorated. It would take Mrs. Brightwell almost a whole month to get ready. She complained about it sometimes but I think deep down inside she loved putting gravestones in her front lawn and flying a ghost on a zip line down her driveway.

After we saw Elena get on her bus, I felt okay about Atticus getting on his bus, too. I thought it would be safe for me to walk home alone after that.

I watched all the big yellow buses pull away from the school then walked to my crosswalk.

Barney the dinosaur stopped traffic so I could cross the street. It was really our crossing guard in a big purple costume. I passed the mailbox where I always mailed my dad's letters and headed down my street toward home.

I looked up at the clouds as I walked down the sidewalk. They were the big fluffy kind, like the ones we watched on the day Pop-pop told us about our Infinity Year.

Atticus always thought everything would work out— even with people like Elena. He really still believed that something magical would happen to make things okay. It was scary that I had begun to believe it, too. I guess it was that Infinity Year magic building up inside me. It felt good, but what if—

Suddenly, I heard a loud yell coming from behind me. There were thumping feet, gaining on me fast.

I froze.

"I'm gonna get you!" the voice called out.

I couldn't move. I was so scared that I couldn't even turn around. Whatever Elena had planned was happening now and Atticus wasn't with me. I was completely alone.

Princess Leia would do something. She wouldn't just stand there. She would whirl around in her flowing white gown and face her enemies. She would not be afraid.

I was no Princess Leia.

The thumping feet got closer. The yelling grew louder.

I closed my eyes and expected the worst.

And then . . .

. . . they passed me by.

I opened my eyes and saw a group of teen ghosts and goblins running down my street in front of me. They had rushed past without noticing me at all.

Two hours later, I was in the backseat of our car with a little brown paper bag in my lap. There was a perfect caramel apple inside. After re-pinning my side-buns (they'd gotten kind of droopy during the day), Mom was taking me to the Brightwells' house.

The caramel apple came from Mrs. White. She makes caramel apples every Halloween, and I've gotten one every year since I was little. Mrs. White is always my first stop on Halloween night. It's a tradition.

I had already eaten my apple. The one in the bag was for Atticus.

Mom looked at me in the rearview mirror while she was driving. "You okay? You've acted strange ever since you got home from school."

I guess I was a little jumpy. It had been that kind of day. Plus, Chloe lived in Atticus's neighborhood, so a little part of me was afraid I would run into the witches while trick-or-treating. But since Atticus, Kevin, and Adam would be with me, what could they really do?

"I'm okay," I said, nodding.

"M and I will miss you tonight," she said. "We always have to give out the candy by ourselves."

"I bet M's a big help," I said, and smiled at her in the mirror.

"Yes, she is," Mom said, and smiled back.

After she dropped me off at the Brightwells', I watched the ghost fly after her down the driveway as she drove away.

Mrs. Brightwell was dressed up like a black cat with drawn-on whiskers and a long tail. Caroline and her boyfriend, Will, were dressed like a cheerleader and a football player. That would have seemed normal except for the fact that Will was dressed as the cheerleader and Caroline was dressed as the football player.

Caroline and Will were officially taking us trick-or-treating. "Ten-year-olds need supervision," Mrs. Brightwell had said. So all four of us walked down the driveway and waved good-bye to Mrs. Brightwell. As soon as she couldn't see us anymore, Caroline turned to Atticus and handed him her cell phone.

"Call Will's cell if anything happens," she said.

"All right, but you sure you don't want to go to the haunted house with us?" Atticus asked. Our first stop every year was at the Coopers' haunted house. I could tell he wanted Caroline to come, too.

She put her arm around him and pulled him aside. I heard some whispering and by the time they turned around it was determined that Caroline and Will were going to the park at the end of the street to see some of their friends and we would meet them there at the end of trick-or-treating. So much for supervision.

It was getting dark when we separated, and the street was starting to get crowded with zombies and other monsters. We met Adam and Kevin in the line outside the Coopers' garage/haunted house. They let only a few people into the haunted house at a time. It's scary in there and this was the first year we were going inside on our own. Atticus's dad, the spy, came with us last year, but he was off on some secret foreign mission tonight.

My dad took us the year before.

Luke Cooper, who wore a rainbow Afro, opened the side door to the garage (the one that's like a regular door) and the four of us walked in. It was very dark. There was a loud growl beside us and I felt myself grabbing for Atticus's hand.

Someone dressed in a monster mask came up behind us and told us to move forward. We started walking and a flashing light came on making everything look like it was moving in slow motion. A zombie jumped out in front of us and I screamed. The flashing light stopped.

A smaller light came on and shone on a boy who was dressed up like a mad scientist.

"You are now entering the sensory chamber," he said in a spooky voice. "You will feel the intestines of a three-hundred-year-old yak and the brain of Albert Einstein. Blindfolds, please."

He handed us blindfolds and we put them on. We had done this last year. Someone guides you through a little room behind the curtain. In there, you are told to put your hands in weird things that feel like brains and intestines (which are really just spaghetti and rubbery eggs and stuff like that).

I looked at Atticus and he gave me his best you-can-do-it face. I put on my blindfold and someone from behind the curtain guided me inside.

I walked several steps without touching a single brain or body part. I heard a door open in front of me. Someone guided me through. Then I heard a door close behind me.

The ground was soft under my sneakers and the air was fresh on my face. I deduced that I had been taken into the Coopers' backyard. This was different. Last year, the haunted house was only held in the garage.

When I tried to walk forward, a hand on my shoulder held me back.

"You have been brought here tonight to pay for your crimes." The voice came from in front of me. Not too close, but not too far. It sounded weird, kind of like Mr. Peterson's voice had sounded as Darth Vader earlier in the morning.

"For too long you have gotten away with far too much and not paid the price," the voice continued. "Tonight we are here to teach you a lesson. It's time you learned your place, Avalon James."

Okay, that was too weird. I reached up to pull off my blindfold.

"Do not take off the blindfold," the voice called out.

I pulled off the blindfold anyway. I was right. I was outside the back of the Coopers' garage looking into the Coopers' backyard. I was standing right underneath their big tree house.

A flashlight beam suddenly shot into my eyes.

I squinted, trying to see. As my eyes adjusted, I made out two ghosts at the other end of the blinding light. They looked like regular Halloween ghosts wearing cutout sheets that went down to their ankles. But their shoes were showing.

I recognized the shoes on one ghost. I had seen those little black boots on Chloe Martin a hundred times.

This wasn't part of the haunted house. And those weren't ghosts. They were witches.

The dots started connecting in my head. Chloe Martin was good friends with Samantha Cooper, who was a sixth grader, and her brothers were running the haunted house. It was Chloe and Samantha who Adam overheard on the bus. It must have been Samantha who led me out here.

The little black boots told me that Chloe was the silent ghost. So that meant Elena must have been the speaking one.

Which led to a frightening question: Where was Sissy?

I had to get out of there. It was a trap. I started to run but my sneaker got caught in my Princess Leia gown and I fell down. I tried to get up but stepped on my dress again. My gown had turned against me and trapped me right there in the Coopers' backyard.

Then I felt it. All at once. Something was suddenly pouring all over me.

It was coming from above. From the tree house.

It was gallons and gallons. The liquid rained down on me. It was like those witches had a cauldron up there.

There was nothing I could do except wait for it to end.

When it did, I was completely soaked and sitting in a puddle on the ground. I couldn't help but taste it.

Milk.

I was covered in milk. The witches had made a real Milk Monster of me.

That's when the flashlight went out.

And that's when I screamed.

EIGHT

I was so mad at Elena, Chloe, and Sissy. I was so mad. After I screamed, Atticus found me covered in milk in the Coopers' backyard. The girls were long gone and my Princess Leia hair and gown were completely ruined.

Note to self: Infinity Year power DOES NOT help with spilled milk, PERIOD! I should have known when I'd seen Mrs. Brightwell dressed like a black cat that things were going to go bad.

Atticus walked me back to his house and I tried not to cry. It was a low point. I was still soaked when we got back to the Brightwells' house. Atticus brought me inside and I dripped milk all over Mrs. Brightwell's hardwood kitchen floor. While Mrs. Brightwell was trying to call Caroline (and her phone kept ringing in Atticus's pocket), I caught

Hello, there.

My name is Kate.
I was the first person
to check out this book
from the Summerglen
branch of the Fort
Worth Library. It is
the most relatable
book I have ever read.
I cried for about 30
minutes while reading it—
From pages 160 to 212.
You will not regret
checking out this book.
Congratulations on picking
up the Infinity year of
Avalon Fames.
    — Kate, 12

her looking at me. I could see it in her eyes. Mrs. Brightwell was adding another item to her list of *Reasons Not to Like Avalon.*

When my mom picked me up, I told her everything that happened. She called Elena's mom right when we got home. Of course, Elena's mom couldn't believe her angel, Elena, could ever do such a thing. But she would ask her about it when she came home from trick-or-treating.

I knew what would happen next. Elena would deny it. Her mom would believe her. And I couldn't prove anything. So Elena would get away with it.

Argggggh!

I had been willing to end it with Elena. I really had. But this was too much. She had gone too far, and I just couldn't let it go. I had been planning how to get back at her all night, and by recess the next day, I was bursting with ways to get my revenge.

"I'm going to find the biggest spider in the whole town and put it in Elena's backpack," I said venomously. Atticus and I were sitting at the top of the jungle gym (now our regular spot), looking at Elena, Sissy, and Chloe, who were jumping rope by the basketball court. They were acting like nothing had happened the night before.

They were the only ones.

Somehow the whole grade knew. As soon as Mae saw me that morning, she'd asked if it was true. Did I really get a bucketful of milk dumped on me? Later, Augustus Sawyer meowed at me in the lunch line.

"Or maybe I'll do a Jasper Hightower," I continued, glaring at Elena, "and dunk her head in the toilet."

"Avalon," Atticus said.

"What?" I snapped back.

"You can't do any of that," he said. "You have to promise me."

I looked at him. "It's not fair, Atticus! You saw what she did to me!"

"I know it's not fair," he said. "But if you get back at her, she's going to get back at you worse, and it's never going to stop. You've got to be the bigger person and let it go."

I dropped my head and groaned. Didn't he know by now that I was not a bigger person kind of person?

"Plus, you have more important things to do," he went on. "Like winning spelling bees. Like going to the nationals."

"I've got to win the regionals first," I said. I'm always surprised how Atticus can dream bigger for me than I can for myself. "And I haven't actually won a spelling bee yet."

"But you will," Atticus said matter-of-factly. "And who knows what's going to happen with our Infinity Year—"

"Stop it with the Infinity Year, Atticus!" I said, cutting him off. "If there was ever a time when I needed my Infinity power, it was in the Coopers' backyard!"

"Shhhh." Atticus put his fingers up to his lips.

"Why should I be quiet? If I didn't get my power then, there's no such thing as an Infinity Year."

Atticus looked around like he was more concerned about

people overhearing us than about what I had actually said. He was strict about the rule that we could only talk about our Infinity Year with each other. "You have to have faith, Avie," he said quietly. "And who would want to waste their magical power on Elena Maxwell anyway? She isn't worth it. Besides, Pop-pop says people like Elena get what they deserve in the end. That's just how life works."

Maybe he was right. But I wasn't sure I wanted to believe anything Pop-pop had to say right now. I just knew one thing. I would have used up all of my Infinity Year magic on Halloween night if I could have turned Elena into a green slimy slug.

I walked around in a grump for the next three weeks. I didn't do anything bad to Elena. But I really wanted to.

Before I knew it, it was almost time for our family tree presentation. During my grump, I decided that getting random old pictures off the Internet would have to do for my father's side of the family. I found some real good ones, too. The older and crankier the people looked, the better.

Mae and I prepared our posters and came up with links between our families. The most bizarre link of all was that we each had a great-great-grandfather with a glass eye.

Mae has a little brother named Noah who is four. When we worked at her house on the presentation, Noah would get into all our pictures and try to draw on our poster board. This would get Mae really upset and she'd yell for her mom to come and get him. But I can tell Mae really likes her brother. I kind of like Noah, too.

I also kind of like Mae. It's weird to have a girl who's a friend. Because Atticus has always been my best friend, I've never really had a girl friend.

Mae and I never talked about my dad, though—not once since Elena embarrassed me about him in the art room that day. I wondered what Mae thought about my dad being in prison. She was always nice to me, but was she secretly ashamed to have me as a project partner?

The night before our presentation we were at Mae's house rehearsing. When we got to the part about my dad and I had to talk about him, I just looked at her.

I could tell she knew what I meant. "I don't know what to say," I finally said. "Everybody knows about my dad. And Elena . . ." My voice trailed off.

I watched her glue my dad's picture to the bottom space on my family tree chart. "Don't worry," she said. "We'll figure out something."

"Yeah," I said quietly.

She looked at me. "What do you want to say?" she asked.

"I don't know," I said. I really didn't know. How do you explain a thing like that to a bunch of kids who already know the terrible thing you're trying to hide from them?

She pressed her hand across his picture to be sure it was glued on good. "Okay," she said. "When you decide, just let me know."

* * *

I finally decided the next day, right before our presentation. While everybody was getting ready, I told Mae my plan. When we got to my father's picture, I would say: *My father was from California. He met my mom at college and then they moved here after graduation and had me.* Then Mae would talk about her dad right away so nobody would have a chance to really think about what I had said.

It was a simple plan but I thought it might work.

After everybody was ready, Mrs. Jackson called up the first team to the front of the class. The order had been established a week earlier by pulling numbers out of a hat. Me and Mae were going third.

We watched Eva Chang and Marcus Johnson go first. Eva's part of the presentation was perfect. She explained everything and everybody while Marcus stood by with—you guessed it—a finger up his nose.

Augustus Sawyer and Elena were next. Augustus talked about his relatives, who were originally from Georgia, and Elena talked about her great-grandparents, who were from Naples, Italy. She also told us how her father was a big lawyer and how her family was so great. Elena's and Augustus's families didn't have much in common. But who would really know? Augustus didn't get to talk much.

Then it was our turn. We propped our posters up against the blackboard and began. We started with our great-great-grandparents and went from there. We had rehearsed everything, so after Mae spoke about one of her ancestors, I spoke about one of mine. It was all going great until I got to my dad.

I looked at the picture of him on the poster board and remembered the last time we were together before everything changed. It was a Saturday afternoon and we walked up to the Jiffy Freeze together. I held his hand as we passed yard after yard covered in orange, red, and yellow leaves. I remember thinking it was too cold a day for ice cream. The next Monday, my father didn't go to work and two policemen showed up at the front door. He never told me what happened. He just went away.

"Avalon," Mae whispered, and nudged me with her arm.

I had almost forgotten where I was. I had such a deep yearning to be eating a double chocolate fudge ice cream cone with my dad that I almost wasn't there.

I took a breath. "This is my dad," I said. "He was born in California and met my mother at college and they moved here after graduation. And had me." There, I said it.

I looked at Mae. She nodded at me and started to talk. Just like we planned.

But Elena talked quicker.

"And then he went to jail," she called out smugly.

Everybody looked at her.

Then everybody looked at me.

It was horrible.

I looked over at Mrs. Jackson and our eyes met. In that

moment (maybe the longest of my life), I could see that she understood everything. How Elena's outburst had paralyzed me and that I couldn't recover. How if I had been a gazelle in the wild, Elena would have eaten me by now.

Mrs. Jackson was about to intervene when someone else came to my aid instead.

"Yes, he did," I heard Mae say. "Avalon's dad went to jail. Like a lot of our ancestors probably did." I looked at Mae and she smiled at me.

"Do you think Avalon's dad is the only one?" she asked the class. "Who else has someone on their family tree who went to jail? There's got to be somebody."

I saw Marcus giving her question serious consideration. Suddenly, Augustus Sawyer yelled out, "My great-uncle went to jail for fighting in a bar when he was eighteen! My dad told me!"

Everybody laughed.

"See," Mae said. "Any of us could have a jailbird somewhere back in the family tree. Even Elena."

Mae looked straight at Elena in case she had anything to say. She didn't.

"My dad can burp the national anthem," Mae continued. "He should go to jail for that."

I smiled a little. At that moment, Mae was my hero.

As the room filled with laughter, Mrs. Jackson rose from her desk. "Okay, class. Settle down," she said. She looked over at me and Mae and winked at us. "Good job, girls." Then she turned to Elena. Without saying a word, Mrs. Jackson flashed her a warning look. Elena pretended not to notice but I saw it. Clear as day.

We went back to our desks and I practically melted into my seat. I was so relieved it was over. And I was so grateful to Mae. She stood up for me. And Elena backed down.

At lunch, I told Atticus what happened. I wondered how he would feel about somebody else looking out for me. I wondered what he would think about me having another friend.

And you know what? Atticus thought it was great. No surprise. Atticus is just that kind of person.

NINE

Mwent missing the week before Christmas.

It was the first Friday morning of Christmas break and I was still in bed. I heard Mom outside moving our garbage cans to the curb. She was making so much noise.

"Avalon," she yelled as she closed the door and came back inside.

I put my pillow over my head.

"Avalon!" I could hear her walking to my door. "Avalon James, if you don't get out of that bed this very minute, there will be consequences." My mom is big on consequences.

"Mom," I whined, and took the pillow off my head. She hates whining, too.

"I called Mrs. White and said you would be there in

fifteen minutes. So don't be late. She will be watching for you, and if you don't show up on time, she will come get you and tell me and then there will be—"

"—consequences," we said at the very same time.

She looked at me with her don't-mess-with-me-when-I'm-going-to-work face. "Okay?" she said.

"Okay," I said, very unenthusiastically.

She walked out of my bedroom and then looked back in. "And no whining," she said.

GRRRRR.

I heard her grab her keys off the kitchen counter. "See you tonight," she said from down the hall. "And please be good."

"We'll be good. Won't we, M?" M was coming with me to Mrs. White's house. It was all arranged. As I heard Mom's car pull out of the driveway, I rolled over toward M's side of the bed. I thought we could cuddle for five more minutes.

"M," I said. But I didn't see her. She wasn't on the bed. I smiled, though. Because M's yellow ball of yarn was right beside my pillow.

I stretched my arms over my head. "Marm?" I called out as I looked around the room. "Where are you, M? We gotta hurry."

Instead of going straight to look for her, I stayed in bed and closed my eyes. I sent her a message with my mind. *M. Where are you? We have to get ready to go to Mrs. White's.* I concentrated even harder. *M. You need to come to the bed right now.*

I know it sounds weird, but I think my Infinity Year power might be that I can mind-talk to animals.

After the Elena incident, I'd been so upset that I'd almost given up believing I would ever get my Infinity Year power. But I couldn't stop believing. Because of Atticus.

Atticus believed so much in our Infinity Year. He was so excited about his magical power. He just knew it was going to happen. And Pop-pop said that Infinity Year magic only worked if it was shared with your best friend. So if I stopped believing, I'd ruin it for both of us. I wouldn't do that to Atticus.

So, one night, I was lying in bed looking at M, who was lying next to me with her eyes closed. I told her with my mind to open her eyes and she did. I was just goofing around but it gave me an idea. What if she could really hear me through my mind?

I started experimenting to see if it was true and my confidence grew based on empirical evidence. We learned in science that empirical evidence was something you got by observing or experimenting. I did both. My observing led me to the conclusion that, yes, M could hear me through my thoughts.

Here's why:

1. Last week, I hid in my closet with the light out and the door barely cracked and sent out a message for M to find me. Within ten minutes, M was

meowing for me. Within fifteen minutes, M was sitting on my lap.

2. Three days ago, I put out two different snacks in different bowls and placed them at opposite ends of the kitchen. One bowl had tuna fish in it, the other bowl had a chicken liver treat. M likes both of these snacks equally. I sat down in the middle of the kitchen, at an equal distance between each bowl, with M on my lap. With my mind, I told M to go to the tuna bowl first. I thought it very hard. Then I let M go. She headed straight for the tuna fish.

3. Last night, I hid her favorite ball of yellow yarn under my mom's pillow. M hardly ever goes into Mom's room. While we were watching TV, I looked at M and told her where the yarn was. Silently. You know, with my mind. This morning I woke up to find the yellow ball of yarn in bed beside my pillow.

If that isn't empirical evidence, I don't know what is.

But strangely, M hadn't jumped on our bed yet. Why hadn't she gotten my message?

I went to the kitchen and grabbed a Pop-Tart. Then I started looking for her. I went to the usual places: the laundry room, the laundry basket, the litter box. I even looked under the bed.

No M.

That was weird.

As I walked back to my bedroom, I looked out the window into the front yard. Where was Mr. Squirrel? For the past two weeks, this squirrel, who we named Mr. Squirrel, had been driving M crazy from outside the window. He would just tap, tap, tap on the glass until M would be driven so mad she would dive straight into the window after him. M bounced off the glass onto the floor at least five times. It was tragic. Something told me Mr. Squirrel thought it was hilarious.

Where *was* Mr. Squirrel? I looked out into the front yard. Mr. Squirrel was at the window every morning. Why wasn't he there today?

Oh no.

I ran out of my room and out the front door and yelled, "M!"

I stood and waited for my cat to show up. "M!" I yelled again. I didn't care if I woke up the entire neighborhood. Where was my kitty??

I was barefoot and my feet were getting cold. I needed to put on some shoes. I needed to mount a search.

Five minutes later, I was knocking on Mrs. White's door.

"Have you seen M?" I asked as soon as she opened the door. "She's not in the house. I can't find her anywhere."

"Are you all right?" she asked.

I realized that I was breathing real fast and my stomach

was hurting. I ran to the side of Mrs. White's porch and threw up my Pop-Tart into her yard.

Mrs. White came and stood beside me. We both looked down at my little pool of vomit.

"Let's get you inside," she said.

She sat me down at her kitchen table and poured me a glass of ginger ale.

"I think she got out of the house when Mom was taking up the garbage cans," I said. "Mom always leaves the door open when she does that, and M never goes out. But she hates that Mr. Squirrel. She must have gone after him. We have to find her."

"I'm sure Marmalade is around here someplace," Mrs. White said. "That cat doesn't look like the kind to miss a meal. Come dinnertime, I expect she'll show up."

How did she know? M never goes outside without me. What if she'd chased Mr. Squirrel and got lost? What if she doesn't know how to get back to me?

Hey—and did Mrs. White just call my cat fat?

I put my head down on the table. Mrs. White put her hand on my back. Her kitchen smelled of cinnamon.

"Have a sip of ginger ale," she said. "Then I'll help you find her."

We looked for M for the next few hours. We went up and down the street. We knocked on everybody's door. But no M.

By the time my mom got home, I had made up a flyer with M's picture on it.

I put a reward of a hundred dollars on the flyer, but my mom said that was too much. I said nothing was too much for M and we had to put the flyers out that night. She said we would put them out in the morning and that M would probably come home before then.

She didn't.

The next morning, Mom helped me make copies of the flyer and we tacked them up on signs and telephone poles all over our part of town. I waited by the phone all afternoon for somebody to call saying they had found M.

No one called.

By nighttime, I was panicking. I parked myself on a chair in front of my bedroom window and wouldn't move. I was using every ounce of my Infinity Year magical mind power. If she was lost and could hear me with my mind, she might be able to find her way back home.

As I looked out in the dark for some sign of my kitty cat, I heard my mom come into my room and sit on my bed.

"I brought you dinner," she said.

"Okay," I said. I didn't look at her. I wasn't taking my eyes off that window.

"Avalon, you need to eat," Mom said.

"I'll eat later."

I heard her sigh.

We sat there in silence for a couple of minutes. Until my mom exploded.

"Avalon, we have talked about this! So many times! What are you writing him for?"

I looked at my mom. She was holding the letter I had been writing to my dad. I had left it on the bed.

"Mom, that's my letter!" I exclaimed. "That's my private property." I reached for the letter but she pulled it away from me.

"We haven't heard from him since your birthday."

"I know," I said. How could I not know that?

"We are moving ahead without your father," she then said. "That is the plan."

"That's your plan!" I heard myself yelling. "It's not my plan. It's not M's plan. Dad messed up but he's still my dad!"

Mom closed her eyes. She hated talking about him and we hardly ever did anymore. But I didn't care. I didn't have M and I didn't have my dad. M was always, always there for me. And Dad had been there, too. Yeah, he worked a lot but he would always joke around with me. He would help me with my flashcards. He understood me.

Sometimes, I didn't think my mother had a clue.

My mom dropped the letter on my bed. "This is making me tired," she said, and walked out of the room.

Great, I thought as I leaned against the cold window. *Just great*.

* * *

The next day, Atticus came over. I was really glad to see him.

His Aunt Lori and Uncle Kevin had arrived for Christmas and that meant Michael was there, too. Along with the new baby girl who they had named Bridget.

Usually, when Michael came to visit, Atticus didn't have to share his room. But because of Bridget, who needed the extra room, Michael had to sleep in Atticus's room—on the top bunk. I could tell that this was bothering Atticus.

"Has he been mean or anything?" I asked as we walked down the street looking for M.

"No, he's been okay," he said. "He's gotten even taller, though."

Looking back, I think I knew that Atticus wasn't worried about Michael being taller. He was worried about something else. But because I was worried about something else, too, I just couldn't see it.

We looked everywhere. We went in everybody's back-yards. We went up around the school. We even looked behind the Jiffy Freeze.

It was cold. "M must be freezing out there," I said. We were sitting on the curb outside the Jiffy Freeze.

"M has lots of fur," Atticus said. "She'll be all right."

"That darn Mr. Squirrel," I said. I hadn't seen Mr. Squirrel since before the morning M went missing. I knew it was that squirrel's fault.

"We'll find her," Atticus said.

"What if we don't?" I asked.

"We'll find her," he said, and looked at me like he really meant it.

"How do you know?" I asked.

"Come on," he said, and got off the curb. "Let's keep looking."

We looked until it got dark. Until it was time for Atticus to go home. We never found M.

Note to self: Infinity Year power DOES NOT help find the most important cat in the world.

That night was Christmas Eve and Mom and I were finally decorating our Christmas tree. It was awful. Dad wasn't there to put up the ornaments and M wasn't there to pull them down. Mom and I barely talked. We were still mad at each other about the letter. Christmas was the next day and I didn't even care. I just wanted my M back.

Christmas came and it was official: the worst in history. I got a gift from Santa, a gift from my mom, and a gift from Grandma Grace that had come through the mail. Nothing from Dad—but that wasn't even what made Christmas so bad. The gift I wanted was for M to come home. I kept looking at her stocking on the mantel. I knew what was inside it. A new collar, a ball with a bell inside, and a little jar of catnip.

At bedtime, Mom put M's stocking on the pillow beside me and gave me a kiss on the cheek. "I'm sorry," she said. "Merry Christmas, sweetheart."

I wasn't sure if she was sorry about M or sorry about the fight we had. Maybe she was sorry about all of it. I tried to smile but I couldn't. "Merry Christmas," I said. I picked one of M's fur balls off my bedspread and rolled it up in my hand.

"Tomorrow will be a better day," Mom said.

As she switched off my light, I turned over and looked out the window. It was so dark and so cold out there.

Darn that Mr. Squirrel.

TEN

The day after Christmas, I woke to a knock at my window. It wasn't Mr. Squirrel. It was Atticus.

I rubbed my eyes and got out of bed. It was cold and I could tell from the light outside that it was really early. I opened my window. "What are you doing here?" I asked.

He looked at me and didn't say anything, but I could tell something was very wrong.

"Get in," I said, unsnapping the screen on my window. He crawled inside and I quickly shut the window behind him. It was freezing out there.

"What's going on?" I asked. I turned to see him pulling my bedspread around him. His face was all red and he was shivering.

"I rode my bike over," he said through chattering teeth.

"You rode your bike over!" That was crazy. His house was miles away. "Are you okay?" I asked, and sat down beside him. He was clearly not okay.

"I had to get out of there," he said.

"You had to get out of your house?" I asked.

"Yeah," he said.

Then it hit me. "What did he do? What did Michael do to you?"

"He didn't do anything," he mumbled.

Huh? This wasn't making any sense. I looked at Atticus like I was deciphering a puzzle. Finally, I asked, "Atticus, what's wrong?"

He didn't answer. He sat on my bed, still as a stone, and wouldn't even look at me. So, I sat there, too, and waited. Which is hard for me. Because I'm Avalon.

"Remember when we went to the farm before Halloween?" he said. I thought back. Yeah, I remembered. Something had been wrong with him that day, too. Also, it was the day he had lied to me. I had not forgotten that.

I nodded.

"My mom was really upset that morning and I didn't know what to do."

"I remember. It was about a test or something, right?" I asked.

"No, Avie. It wasn't about a test," he said. "I lied to you."

So he really did lie to me. I hadn't imagined it. It hurt a little for him to say it out loud.

"Oh. Okay," I said, trying to act like it wasn't a big deal. "So you lied to me—"

"I never lie to you," he exclaimed. "I never do, Avie. And I'm so sorry because friends don't lie to each other and we are friends. Infinity friends. It's just there's something I've never told you and if I don't tell you now, it will be like lying to you all over again. And I don't know who else to tell, but I can't tell anyone because nobody can know. I don't know what else to do. I can only tell you, Avie. I can only tell you."

He stopped. He was all out of breath. He was almost shaking.

"Okay," I said. "Then tell me."

He looked at me and said, "I wet the bed."

I didn't say anything.

"I'm ten years old and I wet the bed," he said, and dropped his head. "It's not like it happens all the time anymore. It even stopped for a while last year and I thought it was over, but it came back again. And it makes my mom so crazy. It really freaks her out. But I can't help it, Avie. The medicine doesn't even help. And then it happened again this morning—and I totally freaked out. I covered everything up but what if Michael finds out? Oh, gosh, what if he finds out? I had to get out of there. I just couldn't be there. I couldn't . . . I just couldn't, Avie."

Wow. Triple wow.

"I know you probably don't even want to be my friend

anymore it's so embarrassing," he said with a sniff. "I wouldn't blame you."

"Is this why we can never stay over at the farm?" I asked. "Is this why she never lets you sleep over anywhere?"

He nodded. "Yeah."

"Wow," I said out loud this time. "That's so messed up."

"I know," he said.

"So what are we going to do about Michael?" I asked.

"I don't know." Atticus shook his head. "I don't know."

I knew what Atticus was afraid of. It wasn't just that Michael might make fun of him. It was that Michael would know. Michael would know something that almost nobody had known. Not even me.

"It even happened to my dad when he was my age," Atticus said, "but my mom just doesn't get it. He tries to tell her to leave me alone but she doesn't and then it just gets worse. She's gonna freak out when she sees my sheets this morning. If I was there, she'd be freaking out on me right now. And Michael would hear. Everyone would hear."

I had never seen Atticus look desperate before.

"It's going to be okay," I finally said.

He just looked at me. "How do you know?" he asked, like he really needed the answer.

"Because we're pinky friends," I said. "And I just know."

I stuck out my pinky finger. In second grade, we came up with this idea of being pinky friends. Whenever anything bad happened, one of us would stick out our pinky finger to the other. Usually it was Atticus who was sticking his pinky out to me because usually I was the one with something bad happening. We would shake pinky fingers and it would all be okay. We hadn't done it since third grade—when we decided we were too old for pinky shakes.

This morning we were not too old for anything.

He looked at me. I looked at him. He stuck out his pinky finger and we shook.

"Okay, then," he said.

"Okay," I answered.

"And if that doesn't work, I'll talk to him," I said. "Michael's a little scared of me, you know."

Atticus almost smiled, then said, "Yeah, I know."

He wiped his nose on his jacket sleeve and sniffed real loud. He saw M's stocking on my bed and pulled out the collar from inside.

After a long minute, he said, "You know, I had a dream about M last night."

"You did?"

"Yeah. It was really real, too. She was in that shed by the water tower. You know, the one that looks like nobody ever goes in there."

"Was she okay?" I asked.

"Yeah. She was."

He started shaking the ball with the bell inside next to his ear.

"Well, let's go, then," I said.

"Avie, it was just a dream."

"I know," I said. I picked up M's new collar and fastened it around my wrist. "I know," I repeated, and took the collar off again.

I couldn't shake this feeling, though. It was a grand-idea feeling and it was banging to get out.

"Yeah, but what if it wasn't just a dream," I said. "What if somehow, you can see things in your dreams that nobody else can? What if your dream *was* your Infinity Year power?" I paused and let this sink in for a second, then looked at him real hard. "Atticus, what if M really is at the water tower?"

"Come on, Avie. Dreaming is not my Infinity Year power. X-ray vision or flying or something like that—those are magical powers. Not dreaming."

"But how do we know? Atticus, it could be anything! It *could* be dreaming! What if you can dream things that come true? What if that's really your magical power?" A part of me thought it was crazy, too, but I so wanted to believe. I missed M so much. I was willing to try anything.

"Okay," he said. "Why not? I can't get into any worse trouble than I'm already in today."

"Really?" I asked. "Are you sure?"

"Yeah. Let's go to the water tower."

I wasn't sure my mom would think an expedition to the water tower would be a good idea. So instead of using the front door and possibly waking her, Atticus and I snuck out my bedroom window. I grabbed my bike quietly from the garage and joined him on the driveway. I had on two sweaters, my heavy coat, and my reindeer hat. I was still freezing.

It was seven o'clock the day after Christmas, so nobody was on the streets. We rode past the school and down the long main road that led toward town. We took a left onto Duffy Drive and saw the water tower up in the distance. We sped down the street riding side by side like we owned the road.

The water tower has been in our town for something like a hundred years. We pulled onto the gravel road that leads to the tower and parked our bikes at the bottom of it.

Every year at the end of school, some high schoolers climb to the top and spray-paint stuff up there. We looked up and read what they wrote last spring.

Lions Rule!

Mr. Waxberger Stinks

Will ♥ *Caroline*

Will actually climbed up there and spray-painted the last one. Caroline said it was a dumb thing to do, but I think she secretly liked it.

The shed was past the water tower back toward the woods. It was bigger than I had thought. It was really more of a cabin. A dirty, rickety, probably dangerous cabin.

I followed Atticus to the door and he turned the knob. It didn't open at first but he shook the handle a few times and pushed real hard. Finally, the door gave way.

It looked like no one had been inside for about a million years. There were old rusty desks stacked on top of one another, filing cabinets with drawers hanging open, and lots of broken rakes and hoes and shovels scattered all over. In other words, the place was full of old junk. Junk that was covered with at least an inch of dust.

"M," I said as we walked inside. "M, are you here?"

We didn't hear anything. We walked in farther.

"Marmalade!" I said louder.

We waited but M didn't answer. I sat down on a dusty crate and put my head in my hands.

"I knew it was stupid to get my hopes up," I said.

"It wasn't that stupid," Atticus said as he sat down beside me. I looked at him. "Yeah, it was a little stupid," he said.

"I just miss her, you know. I don't know what I'm going to do. She's been gone a whole week. Maybe she's never coming back. Maybe I'll never see her again. I miss her so much, Atticus."

I started to cry. I just couldn't help it. We sat in that horrible shed and Atticus watched me. I must have cried for a whole minute.

"I'm sorry," I finally said, and sniffed. As sad as I was, I remembered that Atticus had come to me with a big problem that morning. I needed to get it together. I sniffed again. "What are we going to do about Michael and your mom?"

"I don't know," he said, his shoulders drooping. "I don't think there's anything I can do."

"Yeah," I said.

"My dad says—" Atticus suddenly stopped talking. His head jerked up. "What was that?"

It was dead silent in the shed for about ten seconds. Then we heard it.

Meow.

We looked at each other. I wiped my eyes and listened harder.

Meow.

There it was again!

I jumped up. "M!" I cried. "M!"

She appeared through a gap in the filing cabinets. She was scraggly-looking and missing part of an ear. It was M, though. It was my kitty.

"M," I said, and ran to her. I picked her up and gave her a big hug. She felt thinner. If I had to tell the truth, like in a courtroom or something, I'd have to admit that M has always been kind of a fat cat. Maybe all that fat had helped her last this long.

I turned to Atticus. "You did it! Your dream was true. You got your magical power!"

"I guess I did," Atticus said. His mouth dropped open like he could hardly believe it.

I held M close and kissed her between the ears. Atticus and I sat back down on the dusty crate and petted M until she started purring. We watched her start to come back to being herself.

Atticus was grinning. "What's so funny?" I asked, grinning back.

"I was starting to doubt. I really was."

I knew what he was talking about. We had been waiting for our Infinity Year powers for so long, he was beginning to think they would never come.

"Me too," I said.

"Yours will come soon, I bet. Anytime now."

"You're probably right." I hadn't told him about my mind-talking with animals yet. Too many things had gotten in the way. And I wasn't really sure about it. "It doesn't even matter right now," I said, rubbing my cheek against M's head. "I'm just so happy to have my M back."

Atticus had a far-off look in his eyes. "I wonder what I'll dream of next," he said. I smiled inside. Atticus was already daydreaming about his future night-dreaming.

As the three of us sat in that cold, dusty, rickety shed, it finally felt like Christmas.

Gently, I wrapped M in my coat. We made our way out of the shed and tucked M carefully in the basket on the front of my bike. She rode in the basket all the way home.

As we headed down my street, Atticus started slowing down. Mrs. Brightwell's car was in my driveway.

We both stopped our bikes. "What do we do?" I asked.

Atticus sighed. "We get this over with."

We parked our bikes in the garage. I gathered up M in my coat and Atticus led the way inside.

Mrs. Brightwell and my mom were sitting at our kitchen table. As soon as they saw us, they were both on their feet.

"Avalon," Mom said.

"Atticus," Mrs. Brightwell said. They said our names at the very same time.

"Where have you been?" Mom asked. She looked mad but I could tell she was actually worried.

"How did you get here?" Mrs. Brightwell asked Atticus. She looked mad and I could tell she was actually mad. Atticus tried to answer but she just kept talking. "What were you thinking riding your bike all the way over here?" she said. "It's freezing out there and you could have been hurt and it's the day after Christmas and—"

"You found her!" Mom suddenly exclaimed. She was looking at M's head peeking out of my coat. "How did you find her?"

Mom took M out of my hands and held her close. I had never seen my mom so happy to see anyone before.

"Atticus found her," I said, smiling.

I looked at Atticus. He was smiling, too.

Mrs. Brightwell was not smiling. She turned and picked up her purse off one of the chairs in the kitchen. "Atticus, we have to go," she said.

I looked at her and she looked at me. Yes, Mrs. Brightwell did not like me. Maybe it was because we lived in the wrong part of town. Maybe it was because my father was in prison.

Or maybe it was just because Atticus liked me.

Whatever it was, it didn't matter. Atticus had told me his secret, and there was nothing she could do about that.

I gave her a look, though. It was a look that said don't mess with my best friend. She may not like that we are best friends. But we are. It didn't matter that we were in separate classes. It didn't matter that we sat at different tables at lunch. We were best friends. And that was something that was never going to end. You know, like infinity.

That's just the way it is, Mrs. Brightwell.

ELEVEN

Atticus had gotten his magical power. There was no denying it. So that meant that Pop-pop was right. This was our Infinity Year.

If it had been some other kind of power, one that didn't help me find M, I might have been a little jealous. But I wasn't jealous. I was curious.

What was my magical power going to be? Was it really talking to animals with my mind or was that a little silly? Atticus's magical power definitely showed up when I needed it most. I wondered if mine would show up like that.

It felt like a big fat mystery.

M was doing much better. She had to stay at the vet on that first night, but then she came home and has been camped out on our bed ever since. Her new collar didn't fit because she had lost so much weight. I have put my mind-talking experiments on hold while she is getting better.

Atticus and I have talked about what we think happened to M many times. We have decided on this version of the story:

Before I got up on that Friday before Christmas, Mr. Squirrel tapped on the window and woke up M. M got mad. This was the morning she decided she wasn't going to take it anymore. When she heard Mom take up the garbage cans, M thought this was her chance. She would go outside—just for a few minutes—and take a swipe at that Mr. Squirrel. Show him who was boss and that sort of thing.

M snuck past the open door and tiptoed through the grass toward my window. Mr. Squirrel heard her, though, and turned around. Their eyes met. Mr. Squirrel has very taunting eyes. So when that squirrel took off through the neighborhood, M could not resist it. She chased after him—all the way to the water tower. Mr. Squirrel climbed up a tree beside the shed and jumped through a broken window that was way up high. M followed him up the tree and jumped through the window, too, but my fat cat couldn't get back out. Mr. Squirrel could, though—and did—leaving my M alone, to die.

That Mr. Squirrel is one evil rotten rodent.

I didn't like thinking about how M might have lost a piece of her ear, so we didn't try to figure that part out. I was okay with that remaining a mystery.

Since the day we found M, Atticus and I hadn't talked

about his secret. Not one time. Whenever I wanted to bring it up, I got the feeling I shouldn't. It was kind of like how Atticus never talked about my dad being in prison—unless I talked about it first. So I decided to be okay with it. If he wanted to talk about it, I figured he would.

School started back up and I geared everything in my life toward one thing. The spelling bee. Ever since the classroom bee, Isabel Fernandez had joined me and Mrs. Jackson on Monday and Wednesday afternoons for our spelling drills. Now that the school bee was only three weeks away, we started meeting on Thursday afternoons, too.

We learned a lot together in the three weeks before the bee. Mrs. Jackson really focused on etymology. That means the origins of words. She told us how most of the words we use today can be traced back to their ancient beginnings. They can come from old French words, old Greek words, even old English words. Our words come from everywhere and everyone.

Over the past couple of months, I had also learned some things about Isabel. Her grandparents live in Ecuador and she goes to visit them every summer with the rest of her family, which includes her parents, three brothers, and two sisters. She has a big family and they can all speak Spanish, so she is very good at spelling words with Spanish origins.

I don't have a big family or speak another language, but I was starting to see that Isabel and I have a few things in common. First, we are both superior spellers. Second, we both have a cat that we absolutely love. Her cat is named Daisy and she showed me a picture of her while we were waiting for Mrs. Jackson one afternoon.

Last, we aren't like the other girls. I've noticed that a lot of girls at school come in groups. There was Elena, Sissy, and Chloe, of course. Then there was Mae, Hannah, and their other friends, Courtney and Emma. Mae was nice to me and we were friends, sort of, but I wasn't part of their circle.

Isabel is like me. We don't hang out with other girls much. We don't have girl friends. We have our spelling. We have our cats. And lucky for me, I have Atticus. I didn't think there was an Atticus in Isabel's life.

The Sunday before the bee, Atticus came over all afternoon to help me prepare. When he was reading the flashcards, sometimes he pronounced the words wrong but I could usually figure out what he meant and spell them correctly anyway.

M sat on my lap or his lap the whole time. She was gaining weight and starting to act like her old self again.

The big bee was on Thursday evening, and Atticus had promised to be there. I didn't know about my mom yet. She had to work and hadn't been able to find someone to cover her shift. She was going to try to get off early but couldn't be sure.

So much for my cheering section.

On Wednesday afternoon, Isabel and I sat across from

Mrs. Jackson for the very last time. Mrs. Jackson quizzed us for about an hour by calling out words from her big spelling book. After Isabel spelled *graffiti* correctly, Mrs. Jackson closed her book and looked at us.

"I think we've done enough," she said.

"Are you sure? Because what if we get asked a word we don't know tomorrow?" I asked, rather nervously.

"That will very likely happen," she said. "But you two have tools now. If you don't know a word, ask the questions about it. That will help you figure it out."

Mrs. Jackson was going to be the moderator at the big bee, so we would be asking her all the spelling questions, just like we did during our drills.

She suddenly smiled. "Just remember to breathe," she said, looking at both of us. "And have fun. Spelling bees are supposed to be fun."

Right.

The Grover Cleveland School-Wide Spelling Bee started on Thursday evening at 7:00 p.m.

I had gone to Isabel's house after school and we kept studying our flashcards until it was time to go back to school for the bee. At 6:15 p.m., we put away our flashcards and gave each other a high five. Isabel Fernandez and Avalon James were ready.

At 6:50 p.m., we entered the Grover Cleveland Lunchroom and Auditorium. It was already starting to fill up with parents and kids in the audience. Isabel's mom took us backstage to join the other spellers. There were thirty-eight of us altogether.

I looked around. There were some really big seventh- and eighth-grade girls and boys we would be competing against. They looked at me and Isabel like we were little kids who were crashing their big-kid party. We sat down together on the stairs that led up to the stage.

That's when Mrs. Jackson showed up. She walked into the backstage area like she was the queen bee herself. Get it? The Queen . . . Bee . . .

She started lining us up to go onstage. The fourth graders were up front, followed by the older grades. I saw Hari Singh run in. Mrs. Jackson saw him, too, and tapped her watch.

"You're late, Mr. Singh," she said, and everyone turned and looked at him. "I was starting to get worried."

Hari smiled and brushed his hair out of his eyes. "No need to worry, Mrs. J," he said. "I wouldn't miss this for the world. W-O-R-L-D."

All the kids laughed. To the spellers of our school, Hari Singh was like a rock star.

As Hari got in line, we heard Mr. Peterson at the microphone on the stage. "Parents, students, guests, can I have your attention, please?"

Everybody in the lunchroom and auditorium got quiet. Mr. Peterson continued. "Welcome to the Sixty-Eighth Annual Grover Cleveland School-Wide Spelling Bee."

We heard clapping and some of the big students behind us in line started stomping their feet.

"As you know, great spelling is a tradition here at Grover Cleveland. Over the years, we have had four spellers from our very own school make it to the National Spelling Bee in Washington, DC. Last spring, our own Hari Singh placed twenty-seventh in the national bee."

There was more clapping and foot stomping. From my spot on the stairs, I could see some of the audience. I saw Hari's parents, Mr. and Mrs. Singh, in the front row. The Singhs are from India. Hari's mom wears colorful dresses called saris that wrap around her all the way down to her feet. She has long black hair and a red dot on her forehead. His dad wears regular clothes and thick black glasses. They both speak with accents because they both grew up in India. Hari grew up here.

I heard Mr. Peterson introduce Mrs. Jackson, the spelling bee faculty sponsor. Then he invited the fourth-grade spellers to the stage.

There were rows of chairs on risers on the stage, each row for a different grade. The fourth graders sat down in chairs on the front row as the audience clapped for them.

Then Mr. Peterson called us, the fifth graders. As I walked onto the stage, I felt for the lucky acorn Atticus had given me that was buried in my pocket. I looked out and was surprised how full the auditorium was. All those applauding people made it suddenly more real.

Then came the older grades. When Hari appeared, there was the biggest roar from the crowd yet. I watched him leap up the risers to the seventh-grade row and sit down. I saw him look at his parents, for just a second, and smile. Then he went back to being cool again.

I looked out at the audience for my mom. I couldn't see her. I saw Atticus, though. He was sitting with Caroline and Will in the second row. He smiled and nodded at me, which should have calmed me down but it didn't. I forced a half smile back at him.

Farther back in the audience, I saw Elena sitting with her family. Her older brother, Mark, was in the bee, too. Mark was in eighth grade. I'd never really met him but he seemed nicer than his sister.

I saw an empty seat at the end of one row in the audience and imagined it was reserved for my dad. What if he was somehow magically invisible and sitting there right now? If I needed help, he could secretly mind-talk to me how to spell any word. It felt like an Infinity Year wish that was too good to be true.

The spelling bee was soon underway. It was a lot like our classroom bee—only bigger. When it was your turn to spell, you had to walk up to a microphone at the front of the stage and spell your word to the audience. There were two microphones at the front of the stage. One was higher for the bigger kids and the other was lower for the littler kids.

Mrs. Jackson sat in front of another microphone at a table to the side of the stage and moderated. That means she really ran the whole show. She was there to give us our words, answer our questions, and smile at us encouragingly. She was also the one who would be ringing the bell.

Mrs. Jackson had explained that in this bee, when you got a word wrong, the bell would ring and you would have to leave the stage. In the end, there would only be two spellers left on the whole stage together.

The eighth graders were each called up first. Mrs. Jackson planned it this way so that the younger kids wouldn't be so nervous. Then there were the seventh graders and Hari Singh, who, of course, spelled his word right. By the time the sixth graders were spelling, my palms were sweaty. When the first fifth grader, Aubrey Izurieta, walked to the microphone, my mouth was so dry I could hardly swallow.

Aubrey spelled her word correctly and sat back down again. Then it was Isabel's turn. She walked to the microphone and was asked to spell the word *conundrum*. Isabel asked all the questions we were supposed to ask and then spelled *conundrum* right. Suddenly, her ponytail swung around and she was bouncing back to her seat.

I wasn't ready.

"Avalon James," Mrs. Jackson said over the microphone.

I didn't move. I sat there staring out at the audience.

"Go, Avalon," I heard Isabel whisper in my ear.

"Avalon," Mrs. Jackson said again. She said it nice, though.

I looked at her and she smiled at me—like it was all going to be okay.

I took a breath and got out of my seat. And walked to the littler kid microphone.

"*Scrupulous*," Mrs. Jackson said.

I cleared my throat. "Scrupulous," I said quietly into the microphone. I looked out at all the faces in the audience that were looking back at me. I couldn't remember the questions to ask. I couldn't remember anything. I couldn't even see the word in my head.

I looked at Atticus in the second row. He looked really concerned—like he was afraid I was going to throw up or something. Maybe I *was* going to throw up. Then I couldn't help but look at Elena. Her eyes were all squinty and happy. If I threw up in front of everyone right now, it would make her year.

Finally, my eyes settled on Hari's mom. I wondered why she had a red dot on her forehead. I wondered why she dressed different from the other moms. And I wondered why she was looking at me that way.

It wasn't a mean look or a nice look. It was a firm look. It said, "Get yourself together, kid. You can do this."

It reminded me of Hari.

That's when something wonderful happened. I remembered what Hari told me after the classroom bee in October. "It's all about you and the words," he had said. "Don't let anybody else get in your head."

I felt myself starting to smile inside. Because I realized I had let the whole audience inside my head. With all of them in there, my word was impossible to see.

Hari was right. It has always been about the words and me. Other than M and Atticus, the words were my best friends. They were always with me.

And just like that, the audience got out of my head. It was like I was standing alone on that stage.

Just me and the word.

"Scrupulous," I said. "S-C-R-U-P-U-L-O-U-S," I spelled. "Scrupulous."

"Correct," Mrs. Jackson said. I had forgotten to ask any of the questions, but I spelled the word right anyway.

The audience clapped. There was a loud roar from the second row. Atticus let out a whoop and Will whistled through his fingers. Relieved, I walked back to my chair.

By the fourth round, Isabel was out. She misspelled the word *insouciant*. Her shoulders jerked up when she heard the bell ring. Sadly, I watched as Isabel walked away from the microphone. She exited the stage where her mother suddenly appeared and gave her a hug.

Hari was good at all the questions. He asked about word origins and definitions and parts of speech. Somehow he always made the audience laugh. I looked at his mother every time he spelled. She seemed to hold her breath until he finished every word. I could tell she would never miss one of his spelling bees.

By the tenth round, the stage was getting empty. There were only three of us left. Hari Singh, a sixth-grade girl named Sierra Ghassemian, and me. We all sat in the front row now. There were no fourth graders left in those chairs. There was only us.

By the time the eleventh round started, it was just Hari and me. He was spelling at the microphone for the bigger kids and I was spelling at the microphone for the littler kids. After he spelled his eleventh-round word, we passed each other on my way to the microphone. He grinned at me and stuck out his hand. I slapped his palm and everyone in the audience laughed.

It went on like that, slapping each other's hands in between words, until we got to round eighteen.

It was a silent-letter word that did me in. The first *h* in *diphthong* is silent. Who knew? What's crazy is that *diphthong* is a word about words. It's a word that I had seen before. It's a word from the Greek to the Latin to the French to the English. It's a word I should have known how to spell.

But I didn't.

The bell rang and I took my seat. The only way I could win now was for Hari to spell his word incorrectly. There was very little chance of that.

I looked at the empty chair in the audience—the one my invisible father was sitting in. I was feeling so happy, even though I knew I was about to lose to Hari, and I realized two things. First, that my dad would be happy for me, too, if he were here. And second, that he *wasn't* here and it was no use pretending that he was. So I had a little mind-talk with him. I told him I hoped he was proud of me. I told him I was sorry I didn't win. And I told him I wasn't going to write him any letters anymore. I knew he probably liked getting my letters, but it hurt too much that he stopped answering. It made me feel bad and I didn't want to feel bad anymore. I wanted to feel like I was feeling on that stage all the time.

I watched my invisible dad disappear as Hari walked to the microphone. His word was *doppelgänger*. He spelled it correctly.

Hari Singh won the bee.

Everyone started clapping. Hari was once again our spelling champ. As the whole audience yelled for Hari, I walked off the stage. I missed my word. It was time for me to go.

From the side of the stage, I watched Mr. Peterson give Hari the winning spelling trophy. Hari held it over his head and smiled like he had just won the homecoming football game.

Mr. Peterson finally put up his hands to quiet down the audience. He leaned into the microphone and said, "And now I'd like to congratulate our runner-up, fifth grader Avalon James."

He turned around and saw I was no longer on the stage.

"Avalon?" he said. Everyone began murmuring. I saw Mr. Peterson look at Mrs. Jackson and then I saw Mrs. Jackson point toward me.

"There you are," Mr. Peterson said with a big smile. "Come back up here, Avalon."

As I walked back onto the stage, the audience started clapping. I looked out at all the people and couldn't help but smile. Suddenly, everyone in the auditorium (except probably Elena) was standing up and cheering for me.

It was so weird. I didn't understand at first. I had been so busy spelling, I had forgotten what coming in second place meant.

"Avalon," Mr. Peterson said. "There's only one person I know who did as well as you did in their first spelling bee, and that was Mr. Hari Singh. You should be very proud of your achievement today." There was more clapping.

"Go, Avie," I heard Will yell. Then I looked at Atticus. He was on top of his chair cheering for me. Then I saw my mom. She was standing next to them. She had made it. She was there.

"Avalon James," Mr. Peterson continued, "I present you with our second-place plaque and am proud to announce that you and Harinder Singh will be representing Grover Cleveland K–8 School at the Regional Spelling Bee in April. Congratulations!"

It was really happening. Hari and I were going to the regional bee.

TWELVE

The next week there was a picture of me and Hari on the front page of the *Arcadia Weekly Herald*.

Mrs. Jackson was so proud of us. I could tell she was really proud of me. After the bee, she called me over to her moderator chair. "See, I wasn't wrong about you," she said so nobody else could hear. "I can always pick 'em." She winked at me. "You've got great potential, Avalon James."

Great potential. That's what they used to say about my dad.

Now, I knew the regional bee would be the end for me. At least for this year. Hari would win and Hari would go to the nationals. But I didn't care. I was so excited about going to the regionals that I could hardly stand it. I would get to watch everything Hari did. I would get to learn from the best. I would get the chance of a lifetime.

That night, after the bee, M and I sat on our bed and looked at the plaque I won. I read the words that were etched into the gold metal out loud to her. "Runner-up. Grover Cleveland School-Wide Spelling Bee." Then I pointed to the blank space under the words. "That's where they're going to put my name, M," I told her. I was supposed to bring my plaque back to school on Monday so it could be engraved, but Hari and I were allowed to take our trophies home until then.

M purred extra loud so I could tell she was extra happy for me.

Next to my plaque sat an unfinished letter to my dad. I'd started it before the bee. It had a blank space near the bottom just like my plaque did. I'd been saving that space to tell him how I did.

There was a knock on my door and my mom walked in before I could hide the letter. I didn't look at her as she sat down on the side of my bed.

"You going to tell him how great you did?" she asked.

I looked up at her. After the bee, my mom had run to the side of the stage and given me a big hug. She'd been late, but she'd been there. Now, as I saw her looking at the letter on my bedspread, I didn't know what to say.

"It's okay," my mom said. "Spelling was you and your dad's thing. I know." As I watched her hand touch my letter, she said, "He really missed something tonight. Dad missed something big."

It was the first time she had called him "Dad" since he went away.

In that moment, I realized she wasn't really mad at Dad. She was hurt. Deep-down-in-the-center-of-her-heart hurt. Just like I was.

"You okay?" she asked.

I nodded, still looking at the letter.

"Did you tell M how great you did?"

"Yeah," I said. "I told her everything."

Mom reached out and shook M's little paw. "You would have been very proud of our Avalon tonight, M. She was amazing."

I felt a little smile creep across my face.

"This is the kind of day you will remember your entire life," she said. "Don't let anything or anyone take that away from you."

I nodded again.

"Okay then," she said. "Get some rest." Mom kissed me on the cheek. "Good night, sweetheart."

"'Night, Mom."

As she left my room, I looked at the letter again. I was tired of being so sad. Before I could change my mind, I crumpled up the letter and threw it in the trash.

The next day Atticus met me as usual at recess, but he had a funny look on his face.

"Come with me," he said, all secret-agent-like, and I

followed him to the far edge of the basketball court where nobody was playing.

"Avie," he said very seriously.

"What?" I asked.

"I had another dream."

"You did?"

"Yes, the night before the spelling bee," he said. "I didn't want to say anything because I didn't want to jinx you. And I couldn't say anything about it last night because of all the people around."

"Well, what was it?" I asked, very intrigued.

"I dreamed you were going to the regional bee."

"You did not!"

"I did too."

"That's impossible," I said. I really did think it was impossible. I believed his dream saved M and that was great but could he really dream other things? Actual other things that could come true, too? This was getting spooky.

My puzzled look made Atticus grin. "Avie," he said. "When are you going to finally get it? This really is our Infinity Year. Pop-pop said it. Remember? Infinite possibilities? Maybe nothing's impossible."

Nothing's impossible. I walked around for days with that in my head. Maybe Atticus *was* right. After all, in less than three months, I was actually going to the Regional Spelling Bee.

The spelling drills with Mrs. Jackson started up again on Monday and Wednesday afternoons but now without Isabel.

Isabel was nice about it, though. She gave me a book about Spanish words and said she would help me with them whenever I wanted.

Hari sometimes showed up at our practices. But usually he practiced with his father. They studied together every single night.

As Mrs. Jackson and I worked together, I started to feel different inside. Sure, I wanted to go to the regional bee. I even secretly pictured myself at the national bee in Washington, DC, one day. But those kinds of dreams had always felt far-off to me. Dreams like that came true for people like Hari. Not me.

But why not me? I was a really good speller. Mrs. Jackson believed in me. Atticus believed in me, too. I started to wonder—*What would be possible if I believed in myself?*

Everything I did in those weeks after the school bee was about spelling. Even at recess, I studied. Sometimes Atticus would help but most of the time, I studied on my own.

On one strangely warm day in the middle of February, I sat under the tree behind Mr. Peterson's office with my sleeves rolled up reading through my flashcards. Nearby, Atticus was kicking a soccer ball with Kevin and Adam.

I looked up and saw some girls jumping rope together. Elena was one of them. She looked at me at the very exact time I looked at her. I knew it must have been driving her crazy that I did so great at the spelling bee.

"Avalon."

I turned and saw Mae walking toward me. She was carrying a plastic cup and a paper towel in one hand, and something that looked like stickers in the other.

"Hi, Mae," I said. We hadn't talked much lately, probably because I had been so busy with spelling and we didn't have our Family Tree Project anymore. She sat down beside me.

"I got these tattoos. You want to do them with me?" she asked.

"Sure," I said.

Mae placed the strip of tattoos, which had unicorns on them, and the plastic cup, which was filled with water, on the ground between us. "Hold out your arm," she said.

I rolled up my sleeve further and stretched out my right arm. Mae placed a unicorn on my skin, then dipped the paper towel into the water. Skillfully, she held the unicorn in place and wet the top side of the tattoo with the paper towel.

She pressed her hand against the tattoo and counted very quietly to ten. With the skill of a surgeon, she pulled off the strip, and there, on my arm, rested a perfect white-and-yellow unicorn.

It was great. I smiled and looked up at her. Mae smiled back. "Here," she said, and handed me half the strip. "I love unicorns, don't you?"

I guess. I hadn't really thought about it before. I don't think Atticus and I had ever talked about unicorns. Not even once. "Yeah," I said. "Unicorns are cool."

"My birthday is on March 17," Mae said as we tattooed

ourselves. "My mom is letting me have a slumber party. Hannah and Courtney and Emma are coming. I was wondering if you wanted to come, too."

"Really?" I said. I had never been to a slumber party before.

"Yeah, it'll be fun. And Noah wants to see you. He misses you. He thinks you're deliplicious."

"Deliplicious?" I said.

Mae laughed. "Don't ask. It's his word."

We helped each other pull the little strips off our arms carefully so the unicorns underneath would come off clean. They did. They were perfect.

As we walked back to class, I looked at my arms and thought, *I am covered in unicorn tattoos and I'm going to a slumber party. Who is this new Avalon James?*

The next Saturday the weather was still nice, so Mrs. Brightwell decided it was a good idea to drop me and Atticus off at the farm. She said the fresh air would do us good and my mom agreed. "You need a day outside without spelling and flashcards," my mom had said. But right after another of Granny's fabulous bacon breakfasts (that Atticus didn't eat), it started to rain and we were stuck inside.

For the next three hours, Atticus showed me his new computer app about the *Titanic*. It was a virtual tour of the doomed ocean liner. We looked at the first-class cabins, the second-class cabins, the steerage cabins, the ballroom, the dining room, the upper decks, the lower decks, and the boiler room at least three times.

When it finally stopped raining, I was begging Atticus to go outside.

"Avie, what's wrong with you?" he asked. "Don't you have a sense of history?"

"I am so *Titanic*-ed out," I groaned, and dropped my head on the table.

"I think Avalon's right," Granny said. "You can play on the computer anytime."

"Okay," Atticus said. "But I'm hungry."

Granny made us some sandwiches and put them in little brown bags. It had gotten colder so we put on our coats, grabbed the brown bags, and headed to the hay house. Charlie came, too, and tried to jump on us all the way down the hill.

Atticus was still having dreams and he believed every single one of them was going to come true. Don't get me wrong, I believed it was Atticus's Infinity Year power that helped us find M. And I didn't doubt that he dreamed I was going to the regional bee. But was Iron Man really going to show up for his birthday party?

When we got to the hay house, we settled into our favorite place. Inside, it was warm and we took off our coats. We unpacked our sandwiches and found carrots and chocolate kisses in our paper bags. Today's sandwich was tomato and cheese. Atticus will eat cheese.

So will Charlie.

Before we finished, we heard the truck horn blow and looked out to see Pop-pop drive up with a load of hay bales in the truck bed. "You kids want to come feed those hungry cows with me?" he asked.

"Yeah!" we yelled, and ran out of the hay house. We climbed into the back of the truck and sat on top of the bales of hay.

"You in there good?" Pop-pop hollered back to us.

"We're good," Atticus yelled. Then Pop-pop took off toward the front pasture.

The front pasture is down the hill from the farmhouse— on the front side. As we rode along the dirt road from the barn to the pasture, Charlie chased us all the way. All the cows started mooing when they saw us and the hay coming. When we got to the pasture gate, Pop-pop stopped the truck, got out, opened the gate, got back in, drove through the gate, got out again, closed the gate, and got back in the truck. That's what he has to do every single time.

Pop-pop drove the truck into the middle of the pasture and all the cows followed us. They sure were hungry. Pop-pop climbed into the truck bed with us and started cutting the strings off the hay bales with his pocketknife. He's always careful to get all the strings off so that the cows won't swallow them.

Atticus and I started picking up loose hay squares and

throwing them into the pasture. We had done this job many times before. We were supposed to throw them as far as we could so that all the cows could have at least one piece of hay all to themselves. Pop-pop could throw the farthest, and sometimes he accidentally-on-purpose would throw one right on top of a cow's head. It wouldn't hurt or anything and the cow would shake off her hay hat after a while, but it was always funny.

"Dang blast dog," Pop-pop suddenly said.

We looked over and saw Charlie running all around Frank the bull, who was trying to eat his hay. Charlie was barking at Frank and running between his legs.

"Charlie, you are about to get in some big trouble. You leave that bull alone," Pop-pop yelled.

Charlie is not good at listening, and Pop-pop is not good at not being listened to. Pop-pop jumped out of the truck and walked through the cows on his way to Frank and Charlie.

"Charlie, I mean it." As Pop-pop got closer, Charlie got the message and ran away from him. That left Pop-pop standing right in front of Frank the bull.

Atticus and I watched as the bull and the farmer looked each other in the eye. Pop-pop always said that bulls, even Frank, were unpredictable, but none of the farm animals ever seemed unpredictable around Pop-pop to me. Granny said he had a way with animals. It was like they had an understanding.

I thought about Pop-pop and his Infinity Year. I wondered if his magical power when he was ten had anything to do with animals.

"Look," said Atticus. We watched as Pop-pop stepped forward and touched Frank right on the nose. "That's a good boy," we heard him say. Then Pop-pop backed away and left the bull alone.

"I want to do that," Atticus said. He was about to jump out of the truck when I grabbed him by the back of his pants.

"No," I said. "Pop-pop, tell Atticus he can't do that."

"Atticus, you can't do that," Pop-pop said, and got back in the truck. As we drove toward the pasture gate, I saw the look in Atticus's eyes, though. It said he still thought that big Frank was the same as little Frank.

Me and Pop-pop knew better.

THIRTEEN

It was March 17, Mae's birthday. The day I realized that apparently my Infinity Year power was being unlucky.

All day I had been getting ready for her slumber party. I had my backpack with my toothbrush and toothpaste inside along with my pajamas and my hairbrush and some clothes to wear the next day. I also rolled up my sleeping bag and got it ready because we were going to be sleeping on the floor in Mae's living room that night.

I had gotten Mae a gift, too. Mae had pierced ears and she liked silver things, so I got her a pair of little silver hoops from the Earring Hut at the mall.

Since I was going to be out all night, Mom decided to work an overnight shift and drop me off early at Mae's house on her way to the hospital. I was the first one there.

Mae and her mom were still getting things ready for the party so it became my job to play with Noah, which was fine because I get along well with boys. Noah took me upstairs to his train set that was in his bedroom and told me what he wanted to add.

1. An elevated rail to go over the buildings he had.
2. A bridge to go over the river he had.
3. Three freight cars filled with the sheep and pigs and cows he had.
4. And a new mustache on the conductor he had.

I am somewhat of a train expert from all the time I spent with Atticus and his train sets. So Noah had come to the right person.

We had just finished the elevated rail and were starting work on the bridge when Mrs. Bearman walked in. "Avalon, the other girls are here. You don't have to keep doing this."

"Mom, no!" Noah yelled. "Let Avie stay. Look what we did. It's really great. Avie is really good at trains."

Mrs. Bearman smiled at me. She's a nice mom. I could tell. I liked her from the minute we started the Family Tree Project. "It's very good," she said with a little laugh. She came over and looked at our train construction more closely. "In fact, if I do say so, this may be your best train work yet."

Noah smiled really big. "Yeah, it's the best one!"

"But we're going to take a break. Mae's party is starting. Maybe Avalon will come back and help you finish it a little later," she said. "Would that be okay, Avalon?"

"Sure," I said, and turned to Noah. "We'll get it all done. I promise."

"And Hannah's here, Noah," Mrs. Bearman said. "She wants to see you, too."

"Okay," Noah said, but I could tell he wasn't very happy. I reached out my hand and he took it. "Come on, let's go," I said, and gave him a smile.

It was weird walking in on Hannah, Courtney, Emma, and Mae. They were all in the kitchen picking out beads for a jewelry project we were going to do. I wasn't sure making jewelry was going to be my kind of thing. I was probably much better at train building.

Hannah is very pretty and has very long blond hair. Mae and Hannah have been best friends forever. I think Hannah is going to grow up to be just like Caroline. Courtney has red hair and lots of freckles. She plays soccer and ice-skates. She is very athletic but also very small. Emma has crazy wild hair and she wears dresses all the time. She also wears rings on all her fingers and always carries a little purse.

Mae had just gotten her hair cut for her birthday and was wearing a brand-new outfit. She looked right at home with the other girls.

"Mae, you should see what Noah and Avalon have done," Mrs. Bearman said as we walked into the kitchen.

Mae smiled. The other girls did, too. "Avalon, we're making necklaces," said Hannah. "Come get some string."

And just like that, I was part of the slumber party.

It was a fun night. We made necklaces and bracelets and I was pretty good at it after all. Then we had tacos and birthday cake and gave Mae her presents. I could tell she really liked the earrings I bought her.

When we were getting ready to watch a movie, Mrs. Bearman came up to me and whispered, "Do you mind coming upstairs and helping Noah finish the train set? He just won't go to bed unless you come see him."

That was okay with me. I had already seen the movie anyway. I followed Mrs. Bearman upstairs and it took only half an hour for Noah and me to finish the bridge, load up the animals, and get a new mustache for Conductor Bill. I finished by reading him a story.

"I'm glad you're Mae's friend," Noah said as I closed the book. "You should come sleep over every weekend."

I smiled and thought it might be nice having a little brother.

While Noah was falling asleep, Mrs. Bearman came in and thanked me. I went back downstairs and curled up in my sleeping bag next to the other girls. We watched the rest of the movie, ate lots of popcorn, and then told stories until really late. At some point, we must have all fallen asleep.

If I had just slept through the night, what happened next would not have happened. And my Infinity Year power might not have been being so unlucky.

But I did not sleep through the night. I woke up. Actually, Mae woke me. She needed my help. Noah had wet the bed.

I followed Mae and Noah upstairs. We were being quiet so we wouldn't wake anyone else up. When we shut the door to his bedroom, Noah started crying.

Mae kneeled down in front of him. "You want me to go get Mom?" she asked.

"No," Noah said. "Just you and Avie."

"Okay," Mae said. She took off his wet clothes, cleaned him up, and helped him put on some clean underwear. Then she pulled the sheets off his bed and wiped off the plastic mattress cover that was underneath. I could tell this wasn't the first time Mae had done this.

She handed me some clean pajamas. "Could you put these on him while I go get some new sheets?" she asked.

"Sure," I said as Mae picked up the old sheets and left the room, closing the door partway behind her.

I looked at Noah. I could tell how embarrassed he was. "Hands up," I said, and put his pajama shirt over his head. I got his arms through the sleeves and then started working on his pants.

"I'm sorry, Avie," he said.

"Why are you sorry? There's nothing to be sorry about."

"Only little babies wet the bed."

"That's not true."

"Yes, it is," he said.

"No, it's not," I said.

"Yes, it is." I watched as his mouth turned into a giant pout.

I pulled up his pants and sat him on the chair across from the bed. "Let me tell you something, Noah," I said, and stared him straight in the eyes. "There's nothing wrong with you."

He looked away. He didn't believe me.

"I know what I'm talking about, Noah," I said. "I do. My best friend still wets the bed. And he's going to be eleven soon."

Noah looked at me. "Really?"

"Really," I said.

"Atticus wets the bed?"

It was Mae's voice. I turned and saw her standing at the door with fresh sheets in her hands.

I so wanted to deny it, to tell Mae I was kidding, that of course Atticus didn't wet the bed. But I looked at Noah and knew I couldn't take it back now.

"Yeah," I said to Mae. "I was telling Noah that he had nothing to be sorry about, that there's nothing wrong with him."

"That's right," Mae said, crossing to the bed and smiling at her brother. She and I made Noah's bed, and all the time I felt a knot growing in my stomach. Mae knew Atticus's secret and it was my fault. By the time Noah was finally asleep and we tiptoed out of his room, I was freaking out inside.

"Mae," I whispered as we walked back into the living room, where the other girls were still sleeping.

"What's wrong, Avalon?" she asked. She acted like she genuinely didn't know.

"You can't tell anybody," I said. "Atticus would be so upset."

"Oh, you mean about Atticus wetting the bed?" Mae said.

"Yes," I said, whispering even more softly.

"Don't worry," she said. "I would never do that. Especially after you helped me with Noah. It will be our secret. Okay?"

"Really?" I asked.

"Yeah. For sure. You can count on me."

I let out a sigh. "Thanks," I said. "Thanks, Mae."

She smiled at me. I knew she was telling the truth. I crawled into my sleeping bag and sighed.

Whew. That was a close one.

Monday came quick. The slumber party had been a big success and M was really glad to see me when I got home the next day. Atticus had been at the farm over the weekend so we hadn't talked. I thought about telling him what happened with Mae and Noah but I decided not to. I knew Mae wouldn't say anything. I really thought it would be okay.

By recess, the day had been like any other day. I was sitting under my regular tree waiting for Atticus to arrive when I saw Elena running toward me.

That was alarming. Elena rarely ran toward me. She was out of breath when she reached me but started talking anyway.

I couldn't believe what she said.

"Your boyfriend wets the bed!" she blurted out.

"What?" I said, trying to pretend like I didn't know what she was talking about.

"You know, Atticus, your boyfriend who thinks he's so great. He wets the bed. It's all over school. Didn't you know?"

"No, he doesn't," I lied. But not well enough.

"Yes, he does. I can see it on your face," she said through a wicked grin. "I knew if I asked you I would know for sure. Thanks." She turned and looked across the playground. "Sissy!" she yelled. "It's true." She ran off toward her equally evil friend.

Atticus's secret was out. What was I going to do?

I looked for Mae, but didn't see her anywhere. I had believed her. She said I could count on her. How could she have done this to me?

None of that mattered now.

Atticus's class was coming out to recess. They were walking single file through the double doors that led out to the recess area.

We saw each other at the very exact same time. He walked up to me, looked me in the eye, and didn't say a word. Then he walked away.

"Atticus!" I said, but he didn't stop. I heard some girls giggling and pointing at him as he passed by. I didn't know what to say. I didn't know what to do.

I'd just lost the best friend I ever had.

FOURTEEN

Frank Neuhauser won the first National Spelling Bee. He was born in 1913—the year after the *Titanic* sank—and died almost a hundred years later. He won by correctly spelling the word *gladiolus*, which is defined as an iridaceous plant with swordlike leaves and often brightly colored flower spikes. It comes from the Latin word *gladius*, which means "sword."

Frank was eleven years old when he became the first champion. It happened on a June day in Washington, DC, in 1925. After he defeated the eight other finalists, he was congratulated by President Calvin Coolidge and awarded five hundred dollars in gold and a bicycle. When Frank returned to his hometown of Louisville, Kentucky, the townspeople

threw him a ticker-tape parade. They also gave him a bou-
quet of gladioli.

The regional bee was in two weeks. It was going to take place
in the capital, over an hour away, and Mom was coming with
me. The Singhs had invited us to join them for dinner after the
bee. I expected the dinner was really going to be a victory cele-
bration for Hari. I'm sure that's what his parents expected, too.

It would have been the best time of my life if only Atticus
had been speaking to me.

The past couple of weeks had been horrible. I tried to talk
to him over and over again. But he wouldn't even look at me.
Every time I called him, Mrs. Brightwell (with a hint of glee
in her voice) told me he couldn't talk right then. At lunch,
Atticus started sitting in the middle of the Ms. Smith table, as
far away from me as humanly possible. At recess, he played
baseball and kickball and zombie with the boys.

It wasn't Mae who leaked his secret. It was Hannah. She
overheard us talking about it when we came back to the living room after taking care of Noah. We thought Hannah
was sleeping, but clearly, she was not. Mae found out that
Hannah told her friend Scarlett Murphy about Atticus, and
since Scarlett is the blabbermouth of fifth grade, it went
viral. Mae felt terrible about it and even tried to talk to
Atticus. He wouldn't listen to her, either.

I told my mom everything. Well, everything except what
his secret was. Even though, because of me, it wouldn't be

hard for her to find out. My mom came up with the idea to call Caroline. So I did. I told her what happened and Caroline listened. She told me she would talk to Atticus but that maybe I should give him some time. When I hung up the phone, I was relieved to know that at least one of the Brightwells didn't completely hate me.

It was strange not having Atticus to talk to. I didn't remember what that was like. I could talk to Mae and Isabel at recess, and play with them, too, but it wasn't the same. I realized that with a best friend it's the bits in between the talking that are just as important. The bits where you're not talking. Where you're not playing. Where you're not doing anything. You're just being friends.

I started taking the acorn he gave me to school every day. For luck. I needed luck. More luck than was in that little acorn but I kept it with me anyway. If I ever needed a magical power, now was the time.

Spring arrived, and that meant the Grover Cleveland fifth grade was going to the zoo. It was a forty-five-minute bus ride to the city of Kent and the medium-sized zoo there. On the bus, I sat next to Marcus Johnson in the seat behind Sissy and Elena.

Elena and Sissy were talking loudly about this girl and that boy. It didn't take long before they were talking about Atticus. I knew Elena was trying to make me angry and it was working. I watched her ponytail bounce up and down every time the bus hit a pothole, and I wished I had a pair of scissors. If I had, that ponytail would have been mine.

The three buses from Grover Cleveland arrived at the zoo at 10:00 a.m. Atticus and I had been excited about the zoo trip forever. We had been to the zoo before but not on school buses—not on school time. I was so jealous last year when I watched the fifth graders board the zoo bus. Atticus and I saw the whole thing through Ms. Kinney's window. That was when we were in the same class. That was when we were looking forward to going on the zoo trip together.

The bus door opened with that *whoosh* sound it makes, and we started getting off. We lined up in our classroom lines and each line had a line leader for the day. The line leader for Mrs. Jackson's class was Augustus Sawyer, and he thought that was great. He wore a big blue hat with a pirate flag sticking out of it. We couldn't miss him if we tried. Every class had a parent volunteer with them as well. Our parent volunteer was Chloe's mother, Mrs. Martin.

Mrs. Jackson blew a whistle and everybody quieted down. She was standing next to a woman with long blond hair, khaki shorts, and a clipboard.

"Students, this is Miss Heather," Mrs. Jackson said. "She is going to be our zoo guide for the day. Please stay in your class lines and we will proceed into the zoo area."

"Welcome to the zoo, fifth graders!" Miss Heather said, very enthusiastically. "We're going to have a great day! We have so many mammals and birds and reptiles to visit. And I know you all can't wait to see how far we've come on the new gorilla exhibit. It's going to be quite a day!"

Atticus was standing up ahead in the Ms. Smith line. I wondered if he could tell I was looking at him and wouldn't turn around. Mae's friend Emma was standing in front of him. Her last name was Ballard, so she always came before Brightwell in the line. She turned and said something to Atticus and I heard him laugh.

I looked down at the ring I was wearing on my finger. It was silver with a little elephant on it. My dad gave it to me for my eighth birthday but I hadn't worn it for a long time. Then I felt for the acorn in my pocket. It was there. All I needed was a four-leaf clover and I would be set. Mrs. Jackson blew her whistle again and we started moving toward the zoo.

Once we were inside, we were allowed to get out of our lines as long as we all stayed together. Mrs. Mendez was in charge of keeping us in one big group and she was very serious about it. When Marcus ran over to look at the three-toed sloth, Mrs. Mendez went after him and dragged him back by his ear. I guess that was the only snot-free spot she wasn't afraid to touch.

We visited the reptile house and saw an alligator, many snakes, and a very large and old turtle. The turtle was inside a fence all by himself. I stopped and stared at him. He seemed lonely.

In the bird enclosure, we saw flamingos, cranes, and a peacock with the longest feathers I had ever seen. Miss

Heather told us to watch as the peacock opened his feathers like a big fan. It was beautiful. The feathers were all kinds of colors. I looked at Atticus, who was watching with Adam and Kevin. It was the kind of thing Atticus and I would have talked about for days.

Then we went to see the mammals. Everybody liked this part of the zoo trip the most. It was fun to watch them feed the giraffes and rhinoceroses. Miss Heather told us how animal groups had all kinds of interesting and weird names. "You all know that cows come in herds but look at Mr. Rhino over there," she said. We all looked at the huge rhinoceros with the giant horn growing out of his head. "Does anyone know what a bunch of rhinoceroses is called?"

She waited but nobody answered.

"A crash," she said. "A group of rhinos is called a crash of rhinoceroses."

"No way," I heard Augustus say.

"Way," said Miss Heather. "And guess what they call a group of giraffes?" One of the giraffes lifted up his long neck and turned to us as if he were waiting for an answer.

"It's called a tower. A tower of giraffes," she said when no one answered. "A crash of rhinoceroses ran down the hill and crashed into a tower of giraffes. Get it?"

"Tell us some more!" a kid from Mrs. Mendez's class said.

"Okay, there's a zeal of zebras. A cackle of hyenas. An unkindness of ravens and—look over there!"

We looked over at the elephants just in time to see one

of the really big ones blow water out of her trunk. "That's Bessy," Miss Heather said. "And Bessy has been at this zoo for twenty-six years. She is one of our favorites here and Bessy belongs to a parade of elephants. As in, Bessy joined her parade of elephant friends as they marched in the elephant parade down Main Street. Get it?"

We followed the exuberant Miss Heather onward, along the zoo path. She showed us a sleuth of bears and then, a pride of lions.

I walked by myself among the other fifth graders. I saw Mae in her group of Hannah, Courtney, and Emma and wondered what a group of girls would be called. They were laughing and taking pictures of the animals. I knew I could have joined them if I wanted. I just didn't feel like it.

Up ahead, I saw Elena, Sissy, and Chloe. They were always together. They were like the cackle of hyenas we saw. They hunted together and pounced together. A cackle was a good name for the group of them.

Then there was Isabel. She was walking with her eyes in the book she was holding. As far as I could tell, she didn't even know we were at the zoo. In that moment, I realized I wasn't a Mae or an Elena. I was an Isabel. An Isabel without an Atticus.

We followed Miss Heather around the winding path and then she turned to us, very excitedly. "Welcome to the jungles of Africa and our new gorilla exhibit—still under construction but to be completed by next December," Miss

Heather said proudly as we all gathered around. "Have you heard the one about the Girl Scout troop that ran into the troop of gorillas?" She paused for a second, waiting for a response. "Get it?"

"Ha, ha," Adam said from up front. Atticus was standing next to him pointing at a gorilla that was swinging on a tire hung from a tree.

The new part of the gorilla exhibit was very jungle-like. There were lots of trees and plants and several gorillas. It was bright and nice and the animals looked happy there. The old part of the exhibit was not so nice, though. It was behind a big wall of bars and looked like an old rusty gorilla jail. There was only one gorilla in this section. He stood alone behind the bars. He was the biggest gorilla of them all. He had massive shoulders and his back was covered in silver fur.

"Gorillas can live to be fifty years old in captivity," Miss Heather said. "They live in small groups or troops like this one. You can see several females in the new exhibit section and then there's Toby." She pointed to the big gorilla behind the bars. "Toby is our silverback male and he is thirty-five years old," she said. "He has been at our zoo for ten years."

I looked at Toby, who was eating a humongous leaf.

"Gorillas' hands are much like our own," Miss Heather continued. "They have four fingers and an opposable thumb. Just like us. Does anyone know what an opposable thumb is?"

I saw Isabel look up from her book. "A digit that can bend

and wrap around the other digits," she said. Then she looked down at her book again.

"That is correct," Miss Heather said. "Everyone look at your thumbs. See how your thumb can bend in ways that your fingers cannot. See how your thumb can wrap around all the other fingers or digits on your hand. Primates—apes, chimpanzees, gorillas—are a lot like us. They have opposable thumbs to grab hold of things like tools and bananas. They also have opposable toes. Anybody here have an opposable toe?" she asked.

I saw everyone look down at their feet. "No. None of us has an opposable toe," she said with a laugh. "But our ancient relatives did. Over time, we just didn't need them anymore. Some scientists think in thousands of years we won't even have toes. Because we simply won't need them. Who thinks we'd look funny without our toes though?" she asked.

Everybody nodded and laughed. "We would look super funny," Marcus said as he stuck up his foot and wiggled his toes through his sandals.

"Now look at Toby," Miss Heather said. "He has opposable toes on both his feet so that he can grab things with his toes. That way his feet work like another pair of hands. It's pretty great being a gorilla, don't you all think?"

"Yeah!" I heard some fifth graders yell out. Augustus started making gorilla sounds and scratching under his arms like a big monkey with a pirate flag on his head.

Miss Heather ignored him. "Gorillas are often shown on

TV and the movies as aggressive animals but mostly, they are shy and peaceful. In fact, the gorilla is primarily vegetarian."

I looked at Toby. He was a vegetarian just like Atticus. He had the biggest black eyes I had ever seen. They were sad eyes. While the rest of the fifth grade moved to the other side of the exhibit, I stood there staring at the big gorilla.

With the spelling bee and everything that happened with Atticus, I hadn't thought much about mind-talking with animals lately. I had kind of given up on that.

But here I was, at the zoo, staring at a huge gorilla who seemed as lonely and sad as me. We both looked like we had lost our best friend.

I closed my eyes and decided to send him a message.

Toby, I said as loud as I could in my head. *I'm sorry you are so sad. You look like you should be happy and free out in a real jungle. I'm sorry you're here. But I'm glad you're here, too. Because I could use a friend.*

Mind-talking with him made me feel better—even though I knew he probably didn't hear me. And even if he could, it didn't matter now. Only best friends got magical powers during their Infinity Years.

It hit me like a tidal wave. *Only best friends got magical powers during their Infinity Years.*

I didn't have a best friend anymore. I would never get my Infinity Year power.

My eyes began stinging under my eyelids. I had lost Atticus *and* my Infinity Year.

That was a lot to take in. I wasn't sure my little self could manage it. I felt a pang deep in my stomach, so painful I doubted it would ever heal. And then, as I stood there, eyes closed, right there at the gorilla exhibit, I realized something. I had been fooling myself. Magical powers and Infinity Years weren't for girls who betrayed their best friends. Or for girls whose dads were in jail. Of course, Atticus got his power. Atticus was good. He was trustworthy. He was the best best friend you could ever have. No wonder it worked out the way it did.

Note to self: Infinity Year powers DO NOT happen for girls like me.

I sniffed and wiped my nose with the back of my hand. I opened my eyes.

And found out that maybe I was wrong.

I watched as Toby let go of his humongous leaf and grabbed the bars in front of him with both hands. That gorilla was looking right at me.

Both of us just stood there and looked at each other for the longest time. I felt like I was breathing for the first time since I lost Atticus. I knew that even though there was silence between us, Toby and I were mind-talking to each other.

"That gorilla remind you of something?" The words startled me. I turned and saw Elena. She was standing right next to me.

"Or should I say—does that gorilla remind you of somebody else behind bars?" she said in her very mean way.

Yeah, I knew what she meant but I tried to not listen.

"Did you hear me, Avalon James?"

I bit my lip. She needed to quit talking. I saw Chloe and Sissy walk up behind her. The three of them were definitely a cackle.

"Leave me alone," I said. Where were the teachers? I thought. Why wasn't anyone stopping her?

"Sure. No problem," she said, and turned to go. "But—" She wheeled back around, lifted up her camera, and pointed it toward Toby. "Don't you think I should take a picture? We could send it to your dad. You know, from one jailbird to another."

I couldn't help myself. I wrapped my opposable thumb around my unopposable fingers and I punched Elena in the face. Right in front of Toby the gorilla.

Blood was suddenly everywhere. I looked down at my throbbing fist and saw the culprit. My elephant ring. It had cut Elena right across the cheek.

For a second, I just marveled at all the blood. How could I be responsible for all of that? It was the first time I wanted to take a picture all day.

Then Elena touched her face. When she saw the blood on her hand, she started screaming like I had cut off her arm.

Sissy and Chloe started screaming, too. They were pointing at me and yelling for their moms. Everything started moving in slow motion. I looked over at Toby the gorilla. He was still looking at me with his big black eyes.

Miss Heather had said that gorillas were nonviolent creatures. Mostly. Well, I was mostly a nonviolent creature, too. As Mrs. Mendez grabbed my arm and started dragging me away, I hoped that Toby knew that.

The incident required five stitches and a trip to Mr. Peterson's office. Stitches for Elena and Mr. Peterson's office for me. That was when I found out that, like my mom, Mr. Peterson believed in consequences. Big ones.

FIFTEEN

Mr. Peterson's office smelled like coffee and old air. There were bookshelves against the walls filled with books of all description. Kids' books, grown-up books, textbooks—jammed together in spaces that were not built for so much paper. There was a first layer of books on the shelves in the regular way. There were more books stuffed on top of them. Then there were books crazily stacked in front of the other books. It was like a game of Jenga. If you added just one more book, the whole thing might come down.

I could hear Mrs. Mendez talking to Mr. Peterson in the outer office. I couldn't hear exactly what she was saying but the general idea was: *Avalon James is bad.*

After Mrs. Mendez grabbed me at the zoo, I had looked

for Mrs. Jackson, but she was all the way on the other side of the exhibit with most of the other fifth graders. My zoo trip was immediately terminated. Mrs. Mendez took me to the zoo office, where I had to sit in a room all by myself for the rest of the afternoon. In zoo jail.

On the way back to school, I had to sit in the front of the bus right next to Mrs. Mendez. It was terrible. She never spoke to me. All the other kids on the bus were laughing and having fun. Except for Elena. She wasn't there.

When we got back to school, Mrs. Mendez took me directly to Mr. Peterson's office.

I sat in a chair across from Mr. Peterson's desk staring out the big window that looked onto the playground. It was the end of the day but school hadn't let out yet. The fourth graders were still at recess. Another girl was sitting under my tree.

Mr. Peterson walked in and closed the door behind him. "Mrs. Mendez told me what happened at the zoo today," he said, and sat down behind his desk.

I wanted to say, *Mrs. Mendez hates me. She'd say anything to get me in trouble.* But I didn't. I just said, "I know," and looked down at my shoes.

"Can you tell me what happened, Avalon?" he asked.

"Elena said something bad to me," I said quietly. "I couldn't help it."

"Look at me, Avalon," Mr. Peterson said as he leaned forward on his desk. "I know you've had a hard year. I've had my eye on you and am so proud of how you have gotten yourself back on track." Then he looked at me real hard. "But you know we have a no-bullying policy at the school. There are no exceptions."

Bullying? Was he calling me the bully?

"I'm afraid there will have to be consequences," he said.

"But I'm not the bully!" I heard myself saying. "Elena's the bully! She's always been the bully!"

"That may be the case," he said. "But you struck her in the face. She had to go to the hospital. No matter the cause, there is no excuse for one student hitting another student. There is never an excuse for using violence. You could always go to a teacher for help."

Right. Like Mrs. Mendéz would help me when it came to Sissy and her best friend, Elena.

"I will be speaking with Elena as well to get to the bottom of this," he said, and went quiet so I thought he was finished. He wasn't. What happened next came in slow motion. But still, I couldn't stop the words from rolling out of his mouth.

"I'm sorry to do this, Avalon, but I'm afraid you won't be able to compete in the Regional Spelling Bee this year. Behavior like this requires your immediate disqualification."

My mouth went dry.

"Please use the time instead to think about your actions. There are other ways to deal with your anger and you need to learn them. You're a very gifted speller. There will always be another spelling bee next year."

And just like that, I was out of the regional bee.

As I sat in the chair outside Mr. Peterson's office waiting for my mom, I thought about Adam and how he had been sent to Mr. Peterson's office last year for hocking a loogie at Ms. Kinney's blackboard. It looked like he had been crying when he came back to our class. Then it occurred to me— Adam sat on the sidelines during Field Day last spring. And Adam loves Field Day. It's his favorite day of the whole school year.

That must have been Mr. Peterson's loogie-hocking consequence. No Field Day for Adam.

No spelling bee for me.

Half an hour later, my mom picked me up and drove me home. She had to leave work to get me so she wasn't very happy.

By the time we got home, which wasn't long, I had told her the whole story. About how Elena had teased me about Dad. And about how Elena had deserved it.

Mom turned off the car and sat there without opening the car door. I looked at the back of her head and wondered what she was thinking. I wondered if she would be punishing me, too. Then she opened the glove compartment and pulled out a letter.

She handed it to me in the backseat and said, "This came for you yesterday."

I took the letter and looked at it. I recognized the handwriting.

It was a letter from my dad.

As soon as we got inside the house, I ran to my room, closed the door, and jumped on the bed next to M.

I tore open the envelope and began reading my letter.

Dear Avalon,

I know it's been a long time since I've written you and I'm sorry about that. I've kept meaning to write you. I really have, kid. I've got all your letters. They cheer me up every day. When I stopped hearing from you, I thought you might have given up on me. And, maybe you should have. I know I let you down.

Then I got a letter from your mom telling me about how you did so great in the spelling bee. She said you were amazing and how everyone in the school cheered for you. I wish I could have seen it, Avalon. You know I would have been the loudest one there.

She said you are going to the regional bee soon and that I should wish you luck. Your mom always knew spelling was our thing and that I would kick myself if I didn't tell you how proud I am of you. As usual, your mom was right.

There's something else I need to say to you. I was wrong not to write you for so long. You're my favorite person and I never wanted to hurt you. But sweetheart, I was so ashamed. I let you down. I let your mom down. I just couldn't face any of it for a really long time.

What I did at the dealership was wrong, too. I got mad at Mrs. Prescott for not giving me a raise and I decided to get back at her. I'm not saying that she was right. But what I did was stupid. If I had just kept doing a good job, she might have seen it eventually. But even if she didn't, even if she was the Worst Boss Ever, letting my temper get the best of me didn't help. Instead, it ruined everything. And I'm sorry because I know I've ruined a lot of things for you, too.

I'm glad you're not like me, kid. I'm glad you've got a good head on your shoulders and that you're not a hothead like your dad.

Please write me again, Avalon. I want to hear all about the regional bee. I want to hear about everything!

I love you, sweet girl,

Daddy

When I finished the letter, I felt terrible inside. Because I *was* just like my dad. I did something stupid to ruin my life. Just like him. How could anyone ever be proud of me now?

I opened my bedroom door and saw my mom standing in the hall. She was waiting there for me. I ran into her arms like I was a little girl again.

The next day I was back in Mrs. Jackson's class. Elena had a big bandage across her cheek. She was acting all dramatic about it. Whenever anyone asked her to do anything, she'd say, "I can't now. My face hurts."

She was called to Mr. Peterson's office earlier that morning. She was gone for about thirty minutes. I don't know what happened but I doubted there would be any consequences for Elena. There never were.

At lunch, I sat next to Mae at our table. I looked over at the Ms. Smith table where Atticus was sitting with Kevin and Adam. It had been nineteen days since he had stopped being my friend. I wondered what he thought about me hitting Elena. It's the kind of thing he would have warned me about. In general, he was against things like hitting other girls in the face.

Then he turned and we were suddenly looking at each other. It made me feel so much better, looking into that pair of eyes I most liked in the world. I was about to smile when Kevin threw an empty milk carton at him and Atticus turned away.

After school, I stayed behind to talk to Mrs. Jackson. I sat in my spelling chair just like we did in the spelling drills. She was disappointed, I could tell.

"I really wanted you to be the only fifth grader since Hari Singh to go to the regional bee," she said.

"I did, too," I said.

She just looked at me for the longest time, then said, "You want to tell me what happened, Avalon?"

I did. I wanted to tell her everything. But as I looked into her big trusting eyes, I was suddenly so embarrassed. Mrs. Jackson had helped me so much. She had really believed in me.

"I'm sorry," was all I could say. "I'm sorry I let you down."

"You didn't let me down," she said gently. "But I'm afraid you might have let yourself down."

As I walked out of the classroom, I saw Hari in the hallway, leaning against the wall. His dark hair was hanging over one of his eyes.

"Hey, little speller," he said. "You heading out?"

"Yeah," I said.

"Mind if I walk with you?"

We headed down the hall together toward the double doors that led out of the school. Hari walks to school, too. His house is in the opposite direction from mine, though, on the other side of the water tower.

"I guess you heard what happened," I finally said.

"I think everybody has," he said. "You're the news of the whole school."

"Great," I said unhappily.

We walked outside. It was a warm April afternoon. Not a cloud in the sky.

"I'm so mad I'm not going to see you win," I said.

"How do you know I'm going to win?"

"Don't tease me," I said. "Of course you're going to win."

"I'm not teasing," he said. "Spelling can be a game of chance. Especially at the higher levels. Sometimes you just get the wrong word." He looked down at me and grinned. "But I do have a better chance now that you're not going to be there."

"Come on," I said.

"Really," he said. "You're a good speller. You know what you're doing up there. But—"

He stopped like he was wondering if he should say more. So I said, "But what?"

"Being a great speller isn't just about the words. It's about being a super nerd. And super nerds don't let things get in the way of a spelling bee . . ."

"Even if those things have names like Elena," I said, finishing the thought.

"Yeah," he said. "Even that." He looked down the road toward his house. "I guess I better get going, then."

"Okay," I said. "See you later."

I watched as Hari started walking away. "Hari!" I yelled before he got too far.

He turned around, his hair falling across his eyes.

"Good luck in the bee!"

"Thanks, Avalon," he yelled back. He smiled and waved and then started walking again.

A week later, Hari won the regional bee. Everybody knew he would. No matter what he said, spelling was not a game of chance for Hari Singh. It was practically a sure thing.

May had arrived and Atticus had still not said a word to me. I knew I had done a terrible thing and I knew I had hurt him, but hadn't I suffered enough?

His birthday was on May 15. Mrs. Brightwell was very

particular about sending the invitations out on May 1. I went to the mailbox every day to see if mine was there, but it never was.

I was going to miss Atticus's birthday party for the very first time.

The night before the party, I was lying on the bed with M looking up at the ceiling. M was fat again, having fully recovered from the Mr. Squirrel incident. She was curled up right beside me, having hacked up a gigantic fur ball only moments before.

M would be my friend no matter what. M would always invite me to her birthday party.

I looked at my acorn on the bedside table and then I did something I shouldn't have done. I reached into my bedside table drawer and pulled out the postcards.

Every summer, Atticus sent me postcards from the beach. His family always went there for two weeks and Atticus would send me a postcard almost every other day. I laid them out across the bed and looked at them.

There were pictures of waves and piers and roller coasters and beaches. There was even a postcard of Atticus and his family sitting on beach balls across the sand when he was eight. Other than M and my flashcards, Atticus's postcards from the beach were my favorite things.

I turned them over and looked at all the things he wrote. Like how he wouldn't eat lobster one night and how they saw a bunch of dolphins swimming in the ocean one morning.

Every one of them ended the exact same way:

From,

your friend,

Atticus

I looked and looked at the postcards. The more I looked, the more they looked back. They were part of the story of Atticus and me. A story that was over now.

I couldn't stand to be in my room anymore. I put on my sneakers and tiptoed down the hall. It was late and my mom was already asleep so I was careful not to wake her. I went out the garage door and got on my bike and just started riding.

It was a full moon, so I could see where I was going even though I didn't actually know *where* I was going. I rode and rode until my legs hurt. And then I rode some more.

Oh, yeah, I thought when I finally got there. Turns out, I had known where I was going all along.

My bike bounced down the gravel road as I passed the front pasture. Frank raised his head and looked at me. He snorted. I looked up the hill at Granny and Pop-pop's house and all the lights were out. That was okay. I wasn't going to the farmhouse anyway.

I kept riding, down the valley road that led to the barn. When I reached the shed and Atticus's hay house, I got off my bike. I'd never been there by myself at night. It was dark. The mountains looked like monsters. And the bugs, the seeming gazillions of them, were freakishly loud.

What would my mom think? I'd been trying to avoid that question during the whole bike ride. If she woke up right now and found me not in my bed, she wouldn't be mad. She'd be scared. I felt bad about that.

I parked my bike in the back of the shed and crawled inside Atticus's hay house. I curled up in our favorite place. As I fell asleep, I wished more than ever for a magical power. One that would make me disappear so I wouldn't have to hurt anymore.

SIXTEEN

I realized my magical power had not arrived when I felt Charlie licking me awake the next morning. The day of Atticus's birthday.

"Charlie!" It was Pop-pop's voice hollering for the dog. "Get out of there, boy. Got to feed you before the party starts or Granny'll have my hide."

Charlie just kept wagging his tail and licking my face. Finally, I couldn't take it anymore. "Charlie, stop it," I said as loudly and as quietly as I could at the same time.

"Who's in there?" Pop-pop said.

Uh-oh.

"Whoever's in there better come on out," he said in his don't-mess-with-the-farmer voice.

I wasn't sure what to do. I could stay put and let Pop-pop

come find me. But since Pop-pop was the kind of person who sometimes carried a shotgun, I decided I'd better give myself up.

I crawled out of the hay house and put my hands in the air. Pop-pop looked at me like he was seeing a ghost.

"What are you doing here, sprout?" he asked.

And that's when I started crying.

Pop-pop sat me down on a bale of hay and then sat beside me. He patted my back while I kept on crying. There were so many tears in there, I didn't know when it was going to stop. Charlie sat in front of me and stared up at me the whole time. His dumb sad dog eyes made me feel like crying even more.

Finally, when I started sniffing more than crying, Pop-pop asked, "Is it all out?"

"I think so," I said back.

Pop-pop handed me his handkerchief. He always kept a folded white handkerchief in the back pocket of his jeans. I blew and blew my nose in it. "Atticus hates me and I don't know what to do," I said.

"Now, I doubt that," Pop-pop said. "Don't know exactly what happened between the two of you, but I expect you'll work things through. That's what best friends do."

I looked at him through my red, teary eyes. "But I did something bad. I really hurt him, Pop-pop."

"I got one question for you, then." He paused, all serious-like. "Did you mean to hurt him?"

"No!" I said. "I didn't mean to. I was actually trying to do something good, and it all went wrong. It went terribly wrong. You've got to believe me. I'd never want to hurt Atticus. Not ever."

He looked at me long and hard, and then he nodded his head. "That's all I needed to know."

I handed Pop-pop's handkerchief back to him. He folded it up and put it in his back pocket like it had never been used at all. Then he got up and walked to his pickup truck. Charlie, whose head had been resting on my knee, followed him. When they came back, Pop-pop was holding something in his hand.

"Found it this morning on the hill over there. Was going to give it to Atticus today, for luck. But I think you could use it more. Hold out your hand."

I did, and he dropped a perfect green four-leaf clover into my palm. I had never had my own before. It was supposed to bring the luckiest of luck.

I sniffed one more time. "Thanks," I said.

"You're welcome, sprout," he said, and clapped his hands together. We suddenly heard the bell ringing from up the hill. Pop-pop reached in his pocket and pulled out his cell phone. "She hates when I forget to turn this dang thing on." He chuckled. "Guess it's time for me to put out the tables and get ready for that party."

"Oh no," I said. "What am I going to do? Atticus can't see me here. I'm not even invited!"

"Now that is a problem. What do you think? You want to

make a splashy entrance or you want to make like the Invisible Man?"

"Invisible Man, please," I said. No way did I want anyone to know I was there.

"Okay, then. But first things first. You've got to call your mother. She must be worried sick by now."

So that's what we did. We rode up to the farmhouse and I ducked down real low in the front seat. We passed Granny, Mr. and Mrs. Brightwell, Caroline, and Atticus setting up for the party in the front yard. Pop-pop smuggled me into the house through the back porch. He gave me a bag of party snacks and his cell phone and he sent me upstairs.

"Call your mother and I'll be sure nobody comes upstairs," he said.

"Especially Atticus," I said.

"Especially him," he said back.

As I started up the stairs, Pop-pop walked out the front door. "Where have you been?" I heard Granny say from outside. Then the door closed, and I was alone in the farmhouse.

I went into the upstairs bedroom that looked out over the front yard. Through the window, I could see the whole front of the farm. Pop-pop had started setting up tables. Mr. Brightwell was cleaning the grill. Mrs. Brightwell and Caroline were counting out paper cups and plates. Atticus was playing with Charlie.

Atticus looked different. Maybe a little taller, maybe a little older. He was eleven years old, after all. His Infinity Year was over. It was just one more thing that separated us now.

I punched in numbers on Pop-pop's phone and put it to my ear.

My mom answered immediately. "Hello," she said. I could tell she was upset.

"It's me, Mom," I said.

"Avalon, where are you?!" she said, and I thought she might be crying. "I woke up this morning and you were gone. You scared me to death."

"Mom, I'm sorry," I said, full of guilt. "I'm at the farm. I'm okay. I promise."

"How did you get there?" she asked.

"I rode my bike," I said, suddenly realizing how stupid that was. I thought it best not to tell her I did it at midnight.

"I'm coming," she said, ready to hang up the phone.

"No, wait!" I exclaimed. "Mom, it's Atticus's birthday party and I can't let him know I'm here. Could you come after? Please. Pop-pop snuck me upstairs. I promise I won't move."

It was really quiet on the phone while she was thinking about it.

"Please, Mom," I said again.

I heard her blow her nose. "Okay," she said. "We will be talking about this later."

"I know."

"Call me when the party's over," she said.

"I promise," I said, then said good-bye and hung up the phone.

Then I pulled up a chair and started watching Atticus's birthday party. For a while it was almost like I was at the movies. I ate my party snacks and watched the other fifth graders arrive. It seemed like all of Ms. Smith's fifth-grade class was there. It was like no one remembered Atticus's secret. I was glad. That made me feel better.

Nobody saw me staring down at them. I was completely invisible to them. I heard Granny and Mrs. Brightwell come inside to the kitchen every now and then, but nobody came upstairs. It was my own private show.

I watched the scavenger hunt. We had done that last year. Mrs. Brightwell gave everyone maps and they got to go find stuff like rubber swords and glow sticks in hidden places outside. Then there was a three-legged race across the front yard. Me and Atticus had won last year. This year, Atticus came in third with Adam, his new partner.

After that, it was time for lunch. Everybody sat at the long tables that Pop-pop had put out. There were hot dogs and hamburgers and potato chips and baked beans. I knew Atticus's hamburger was really a veggie burger. While he was eating, I saw him grab one potato chip after another and slip them under the table. I imagined Charlie happily eating every one of them.

Then there was birthday cake (Atticus's favorite was chocolate with white icing) and the birthday song. I sang along quietly when Mrs. Brightwell came out of the kitchen carrying the lit-up cake. I watched Atticus make a wish and blow out the candles. I made a wish, too.

After lunch, the adults started cleaning up while all the kids broke off into different groups to play. Charlie was acting crazy, trying to eat up all the fallen hamburgers and hot dogs before Mrs. Brightwell got them in the garbage can. I watched Atticus walk down the hill toward the front pasture with Kevin and Adam. He seemed to be having a good birthday. He didn't seem to be missing me at all.

It wouldn't be long now. The party would be over. My mother would pick me up, and with luck, Atticus would never even know I had been there. I looked at the four-leaf clover Pop-pop had given me. I had carefully put it on the windowsill after I called my mom. Four-leaf clovers were supposed to be lucky but maybe, I was starting to decide, there was no such thing as luck.

But . . .

As luck would have it, I looked up at that very moment. I saw Atticus way down the hill, in front of the gate to the front pasture. He was pointing at Frank the bull. Whatever Atticus was saying, it looked like Kevin and Adam thought it was a fantastic idea.

I knew, even from this distance, that it was not fantastic. I knew Atticus and I knew what he was thinking about doing. I knew those boys were just stupid enough to let him.

And just like that, Atticus was climbing over the fence. He was walking through the pasture toward Frank the bull. Kevin and Adam were cheering him all the way.

There was no time to think. I started to run. I ran down the stairs and out the front door, right into the open. As I flew past Mrs. Brightwell, I saw her head turn and thought I heard her call my name. There was no time to stop, though. No time to tell adults what was happening. There was only time to run.

I'd never gone down the driveway so fast before. My eyes were on Atticus the whole time. He was getting closer and closer to Frank. I could see that he was talking to him.

Didn't Atticus know that he was not like his grandfather? Didn't he know that this was going to end badly?

Apparently not, because Atticus walked right up to Frank and reached out to pet him. Frank's head was down. He was eating grass. He wasn't paying any attention to Atticus until he touched him—right on the forehead.

Frank's head roared up. The big bull snorted. He pawed the ground then lurched forward. Frank butted Atticus right in the stomach.

And Atticus went flying.

I was over the fence by then. I was past Kevin and Adam before they knew what was happening. I was on my way to Atticus, but so was Frank. And there was no doubt in my mind—Frank was going to get there first.

I didn't know what to do. Atticus wasn't my best friend anymore so I didn't have my Infinity Year power. I couldn't save him.

But then I had a crazy thought. What if my Infinity Year *wasn't* over? Just because Atticus was mad at me didn't mean we weren't best friends anymore. He was still *my* best friend. No matter what he thought.

I remembered the zoo and how Toby the gorilla seemed to hear me when I talked to him with my mind. I remembered how M had heard my thoughts, too. And then I felt it. At first, deep inside, like those other times, and then, like a wave cresting and breaking in the ocean, unstoppable and undeniable, I felt my Infinity Year power sweep through me. Huge, powerful, and not about to let my best friend get hurt by some dumb bull.

Frank had reached Atticus now. He was starting to paw at him.

"FRANK!" I yelled.

M had heard me. Toby had heard me. And I knew, I just *knew*, that Frank the bull was going to hear me, too. Once I stopped yelling like an idiot and used my power correctly.

With every ounce of Infinity Year mind-talk power that I had, I told Frank, *Stop it right now! You turn around and look at me!*

And amazingly, Frank did. Without me saying a word, that bull just turned around and looked my way.

Frank was even bigger than Toby and there were no bars

between us. We just stood there staring at each other. Frank was breathing real hard through his big nostrils. I was breathing real hard through my little ones. I saw Atticus on the ground on the other side of Frank. He wasn't moving.

I looked toward the fence and saw Adam's and Kevin's shocked faces. Behind them, Mrs. Brightwell was running down the driveway. She would get to Atticus. She would make sure he was okay. I just had to get that darn bull away from him.

Frank lowered his head and started beating the ground with one of his hooves.

Oh no, I thought. I looked behind me.

I couldn't go back the way I came. Mrs. Brightwell was coming through the gate to rescue Atticus. I had to go the other way—the long way across the pasture to the fence on the other side. It was a football field long. And I knew I wasn't going to be fast enough.

But I didn't care.

"Come on, Frank!" I yelled (this time with my mind *and* my mouth), and started running.

The grass was tall and it slapped at my legs, but I didn't really feel it. I looked back. Frank had taken the bait. He was following me. Good.

Or bad. Because Frank was really fast, and he was starting to charge down the field after me. He looked mad, too. I ran faster, but every time I looked back, he was getting closer. I realized I was not going to make it to the fence in time.

I was not going to outrun Frank the bull.

Frank the bull was going to outrun me.

I don't know if it was because of the four-leaf clover on the windowsill or Atticus's acorn in my pocket, but Luck finally showed his face to me. After all this time. And wouldn't you know it, he looked just like Charlie the dog.

From out of nowhere, that dog darted right between me and that bull. Charlie distracted Frank just long enough for me to make it to the fence. Even though my legs felt full of jelly, I climbed up to the top and looked back just in time to see Atticus being carried out of the pasture.

And just in time to see Frank the bull look at me—like he knew he just got beat by a ten-year-old girl.

I smiled.

Then I fell.

That was the last thing I remembered.

SEVENTEEN

Atticus had a concussion and two broken ribs. That stupid boy was going to live.

The doctors were making him stay in the hospital for the rest of the weekend. Mom said they liked to keep an eye on people with head injuries and Atticus had landed on his head. I had landed on my head, too, when I fell off the fence, but I felt just fine. My mom drove me to the hospital anyway—just to be on the safe side.

Turns out my head was okay. But my heart was still hurting. I asked my mom if we could wait to see Atticus.

We sat in the waiting room for about an hour. I looked at magazines and started picking at the scab that was forming around my elbow. Evidently, I fell on my head *and* my elbow. It was funny how I didn't remember falling off the fence. I *do* remember Charlie licking me, though. And Pop-pop picking me up and carrying me to the farmhouse.

Mrs. Brightwell came into the waiting room to give us an update on Atticus's condition. He was sore and it hurt him to cough, but he was going to be fine. My mom left to get them some coffee but Mrs. Brightwell didn't go anywhere. She stayed right there with me.

That was weird.

"Can I talk to you?" she asked.

"Sure," I said. I watched as she sat down in one of the waiting room chairs across from me.

"I want to thank you for today," she said. "I don't know how you showed up when you did, but you saved my boy. That bull could have killed him. I owe you, Avalon."

"That's okay," I said. She had never talked to me like this before. It was all very strange.

"Avalon, I have to admit something to you," she said. "I need to fess up." She paused before continuing. "When you and Atticus had your falling-out, I was actually relieved. I was. I thought he needed more friends. I thought he needed different friends. I thought that you weren't good for him."

"I know," I said.

She looked surprised, like she didn't expect me to say that. Or to know that. But I did.

"It's always scared me, how you sometimes act before

you think," she continued. "I know it can get you in trouble. And I was afraid it would get Atticus in trouble, too." Mrs. Brightwell cleared her throat, like maybe she was getting choked up, then said, "But here's the thing, Avalon. You didn't think about what you did today. You just did it. You ran in front of that bull without thinking about yourself. You were just going to save Atticus—no matter what happened. And in this case, I'm really glad you did."

After all this time, I finally knew why she didn't like me.

"But—" she added.

Uh-oh.

"I have to tell you I did something that I am now very ashamed of. And I hope you will forgive me." Mrs. Brightwell reached in her purse and pulled out an envelope. She handed it to me. It had my name on it.

It was my invitation to Atticus's birthday party. "I didn't mail it," she said. "Atticus doesn't know. He would be furious with me. And he should be."

I opened the invitation and looked at it. I realized I had been invited to his birthday party all along. There was a note in there, too. I pulled it out and started to read.

> *Dear Avie,*
>
> *It's me. Atticus. Caroline told me what happened. I know it wasn't your fault. It just freaked me out and I got really mad.*
>
> *Please come to my birthday party. It will be fun.*

If you say yes, I will know you want to speak to me again.
So please say yes!
I'm sorry.
Will you still be my best friend?

From,
your best friend,
Atticus

My heart felt much better.

"Today, I realized something, Avalon," Mrs. Brightwell said. "I want Atticus to have lots of friends in his life. But one of them should always be you. He needs you."

I couldn't help but smile a little.

"And I didn't see any of those boys running in there to save him," she said, smiling back at me. "I'm so sorry. I just worry about him too much, I guess."

I was suddenly feeling bolder, like I could ask her anything. So I did. "Why do you worry about him all the time?" I asked.

She looked at me. I could tell she didn't have a good answer. "Because Atticus is the best person I know," I said. "How could you worry about somebody like that? He'll always be okay. And if he's not, he'll have you and me and Caroline to make sure of it." I looked at her real hard—the way Pop-pop had looked at me—and said, "Atticus is Atticus, Mrs. Brightwell. Nobody can ever change that."

She grabbed a tissue out of her handbag and wiped one of

her eyes. I heard her sniff just like her son. Finally, she said, "You want to come see him?"

We walked into Atticus's hospital room together. He had a bandage around his ribs and a big black bruise under his eye. I walked over to the bed.

"Are you all right?" I asked.

"Yeah," he said. "Thanks for saving my life."

"Anytime. You would have done the same for me."

"Yeah. I would have," he said. Then Atticus grinned at me—for the first time in two whole months.

"What's that?" he asked, pointing to the envelope in my hand. I held up the birthday invitation.

"Oh, yeah. It's your birthday invitation. Can you believe I only got it today? That's why I was so late for your party." I was such a good liar sometimes. I looked at Mrs. Brightwell. I could tell she wanted to shake her head at me, but she only smiled. "I think I'll go find your mom and that coffee," she said. "Give you two a chance to catch up."

"Thanks, Mom," Atticus said.

"Thanks, Mrs. Brightwell," I added.

Mrs. Brightwell left the room and it got awfully quiet.

"I'm so sorry, Atticus," I finally said.

"It's okay. I know you didn't mean it. Caroline told me everything. Did you read my letter?" he asked.

I nodded.

"I was just so embarrassed and freaked out," he said. "I kind of lost it."

"I don't blame you," I said. "I would have been mad, too."

"Yeah, but it all worked out."

"What do you mean?"

"It turns out I wasn't the only one. There are a few of us fifth-grade bed wetters and we kind of made a club."

"Really?"

"Really."

"Cool," I said. "So who's in the club?"

Atticus raised his eyebrow at me. "Like I'm going to tell you that?" he said, and grinned. "But it's gotten better, though. Mom and I sort of came to a truce about it. And that helped. Or maybe it was just my Infinity Year that cured me."

He smiled at me and I smiled back. For a moment, we settled in to being best friends again.

Then I said, "I think I got mine. You know—my Infinity Year power. Right there in the pasture."

Atticus beamed. "I know you did. Mom said you ran faster than Frank. She said she couldn't believe that you could run that fast." He tried to lean forward, but I could tell it hurt his ribs. "Remember when you said you didn't want your power to be running fast or anything like that?"

"When did I say that?"

"I don't know. You said it, though."

"Well, I guess I changed my mind," I said. "But it wasn't just the running."

"What was it, then?"

"I spoke to Frank. With my mind."

Atticus looked totally intrigued.

"I told him to follow me, to leave you alone. And he listened to me. And I didn't say a word."

"Whoa," Atticus said. "That's a great power!"

"I know. Right?" Then something occurred to me. "Did you dream about petting Frank before you really did it?"

"How'd you know?"

"Because that's the kind of dumb dream that would get you into this mess," I said. "What happened in the dream anyway?"

"I don't know. I woke up before I actually reached him."

I laughed. That was the stupidest thing I ever heard. It was probably a good thing Atticus's Infinity Year was over. Before one of his dreams actually killed him.

"That's quite a shiner, boy." I turned around and saw Pop-pop standing at the end of Atticus's bed.

"Pop-pop!" Atticus said.

"How are you feeling?" he asked Atticus.

"I'm okay," Atticus said.

Then he looked at me. "And how about you, our little hero?"

I blushed. "I'm okay, too."

"Well, just checking to be sure you both are in one piece," he said. "You had me a little worried this afternoon."

Atticus and I looked at each other and smiled. Then Atticus's eyes got real wide. "Pop-pop!" he exclaimed. "Can you tell us now?"

It took me less than a second to understand what he meant. "Yes, please!" I chimed in. "We want to know about your Infinity Year."

Pop-pop grinned. "Huh," he said. "You want to hear about my magical power."

"Come on," Atticus cried. "I'm eleven. You can tell me now."

Pop-pop looked at me. "Avalon's still ten. I don't know," he said, shaking his head.

"Please!" I said. "Please!"

"All right, then. Today I will make an exception," he said, and looked behind him to be sure nobody else was listening.

"Okay," he said. "My magical power wasn't like my grandpa's. Grandpa Daniel could make himself invisible for most of his tenth year. Being invisible sounded pretty neat to me when I was ten."

"Me too," I said quietly.

"But no, mine was a onetime thing. My best friend, Jimmy, and I were at the lake. It was a spring day, much like today was. We were having fun—like boys will do. There were a bunch of us there. Jimmy and I decided to be hotshots, so we climbed up on some high rocks above the other boys. We were going to jump off into the water. Jimmy jumped first. But instead of jumping, dumb Jimmy thought he should dive in. So he did.

"You kids know you're never supposed to dive into lake water because in most lakes you can't see to the bottom. This lake was no exception. Jimmy dove in but he didn't come up."

"What did you do?" Atticus asked, very concerned for Jimmy.

"I jumped in after him," Pop-pop said. "But once I got under that water, I couldn't see anything. I couldn't see Jimmy. I couldn't see my hand in front of my face. I finally came back to the surface, and Jimmy still hadn't come up for air. And that's when I remembered it was my Infinity Year. I knew there was a magical power somewhere inside me. I was just praying it was going to come out on that very day. So I took in a deep breath and went back down under."

I looked at Atticus. We really did know that Jimmy was going to be okay because he was a grown man now. He was Pop-pop's age. But, still, we were worried.

"I stayed under that water until I found Jimmy and pulled him up," Pop-pop continued. "The other boys said we were down there for a really long time. They were scared we both were drowned."

"But you weren't?" Atticus asked.

"Nope, we weren't," he said, his eyes twinkling. "Funny, I got my magical power for only one afternoon. I was able to hold my breath long enough to save my best friend. That was enough magic to last me a lifetime."

I nodded. I pictured that day on the lake. I saw Pop-pop pulling Jimmy out of the water. "What was Jimmy's magical power?" I asked.

"Jimmy hit his head on a rock," Pop-pop said, then looked at Atticus. "So I'd say Jimmy's magical power was that he lived."

EIGHTEEN

My Infinity Year was ending. Atticus was out of school, still recovering from his concussion, and I was at recess alone. Well, I wasn't really alone, of course. Other than Atticus, the whole fifth grade was there.

I sat on a swing in the corner of the playground with a stack of flashcards in my lap. Even though there was no spelling bee to study for, like Mr. Peterson said, there was always next year. I had decided to be ready.

Mae and Hannah were talking by the jungle gym. Adam and Kevin were dribbling basketballs. Isabel was reading a book under my old tree.

I picked up a flashcard from the top of the pile. I glanced at the word before lifting it over my head and out of view. *Catastrophe.* C-A-T-A-S-T-R-O—I was spelling the word in my head when I felt the flashcard being snatched from my hand.

It was—who else?—Elena. She wheeled around and waved my flashcard in front of my eyes. It was one of those rare occasions when she was alone. No Sissy or Chloe in sight.

"Give it back, Elena," I said from the swing.

"Why should I?" she taunted.

"Because it's mine. Give it back."

"Because it's mine. Give it back," she mimicked.

"I'm serious, Elena!"

"I'm serious, too!"

Whenever they talk about bullies in books or in school, they always say it's because the bully is insecure or scared and that's why they're so mean to everybody. I looked up at Elena. She didn't look insecure. Or scared.

We stared at each other. A fifth-grade playground stand-off. Together but alone. No best friends to come to our aid.

And strangely, I began to feel sad for Elena. She had Sissy and Chloe but they weren't really her friends. They were her followers, her minions. Sissy would never have a magical dream that saved Elena's cat. Chloe wouldn't ever outrun a bull to save her leader's life. No, Elena didn't have friends like that.

Even though Atticus wasn't beside me on the playground, he was always with me in spirit. Unless Elena changed, I knew she would never have that kind of friend.

"Elena?" I finally asked.

"What?" she snapped back.

"Why are you like this?" I didn't say it mad. Really, I didn't. I just wanted to know.

Something changed in her eyes. For a single second, Elena Maxwell didn't look so tough. "Like what?" she asked, and looked at me like she might want an answer.

"Ah, you know," I said, pointing at my flashcard.

"Oh," she said, and looked at the card in her hand. She was quiet for a moment while a crowd started forming around us. Mae and Hannah, Kevin and Adam, Sissy and Chloe and others. All coming to see what Elena would do next. Finally, Elena noticed it, too.

When she saw Sissy and Chloe, I saw the steel return to her eyes. The possibility of a warm fuzzy Elena was over. The return of evil Elena was confirmed.

"Why am I like this?" she spat loudly so everyone could hear. "You mean, TOTALLY AWESOME?!"

It was her big Cruella moment. She smiled and laughed, and her friends joined in. But as usual with Elena, it wasn't enough. She always needed a final flourish. I watched as it came my way.

Elena thrust my flashcard right in front of my face and tore it clean in half.

"Really?" I asked. "Seriously?" As my voice got louder, I could feel the volcano beginning to erupt inside. Atticus may have been there in spirit but he wasn't *actually* there to stop me. What would it matter if I got up from this swing and . . .

That's when I realized it would matter a lot. I was a super nerd. A Spelling Nerd. And I was never going to let somebody like Elena get in my way again.

Would I have done what I did next if Mrs. Jackson wasn't walking up behind Elena? It's uncertain. But in a year of infinite possibilities, it was at least possible.

I stood up in front of the whole fifth grade and held out my stack of flashcards to Elena. "Here," I said. "They're yours. I'm not fighting you anymore."

A hungry look came over Elena's face. Without hesitation, she grabbed all my flashcards and gleefully threw them up in the air. As they rained down upon us, Elena happily whirled around and ran directly into Mrs. Jackson. Who took her directly to Mr. Peterson's office.

And the entire fifth grade at Grover Cleveland K–8— witches excluded—cheered.

The end of my Infinity Year came ten days later. It was the day after the last day of school, which was my birthday. It was also the day of the National Spelling Bee in Washington, DC.

I got two unexpected gifts on my birthday. The first one came when my mom woke me up. She was holding an envelope in her hand.

"What's that?" I asked, rubbing my eyes.

"It's for you," she said, and handed it to me.

I recognized the handwriting on the envelope.

"It came in the mail yesterday," Mom said. "I thought it should be the first thing you opened on your birthday."

I tore open the envelope and pulled out the birthday card. It had a big fat cat on the front with a caption that said, "It's a PURRFECT day for birthday cake." Inside, it said, "Be sure to save me a piece." The card was sweet and funny—like the ones my dad used to give me. But that wasn't the greatest part. It's what he wrote underneath that took my breath away:

I hope you have a wonderful day, Avalon. I'm sorry I'm missing it but we can celebrate when I see you soon. Can't wait to see my sweet girl again!

Happy Birthday.

Love,
Dad

I looked up at my mom, a big question in my eyes.

"We're going to visit him. In two weeks," she said. "Will that work for you?"

I nodded, then reached up and gave my mom a humongous hug. Yes, that would work for me.

I got my other surprise gift later that afternoon. It came from Mrs. Brightwell. Atticus had come over to celebrate my birthday. It was going to be just him, me, and M having birthday cake together and watching the national bee. Mrs. Brightwell didn't leave right away and I thought that was weird. "Avalon," she said. "Atticus and I, along with Caroline and Mr. Brightwell, would like to ask you something."

"Okay," I said, and looked at Atticus. I could tell he was holding something big inside. I looked at his mom again.

"Would you be our guest and come to the beach with us this summer?" she asked. Both she and my mom were smiling at me, waiting for my answer. I turned to Atticus. He knew it was my true-life aim to go to the ocean.

"So, Avie, will you come with us?" he asked, all excited.

I looked at them all and grinned. I think you can guess what I said.

After Mrs. Brightwell left, we ate cake and ice cream and Mom and Atticus sang me the birthday song. Mom took a picture of Atticus and me with my birthday cake and then Atticus, M, and I started watching the National Spelling Bee on TV.

We saw Hari get through round after round. He was so smart. And so funny. And boy, he could spell. In the end, he missed the word *chamaephyte*. It is a word about plants that comes from the Greek. We clapped with the audience on TV as Hari walked off the stage, having placed thirteenth.

As we watched, I realized my Infinity Year was over. I'd turned eleven. A part of me still wondered if Toby the gorilla or Frank the bull had really heard me. But that didn't matter anymore. I think my Infinity Year power was like Pop-pop's.

It came for one magical afternoon and helped me save my best friend. Like Pop-pop, that was all the Infinity magic I would ever need.

I looked over at Atticus. M was sitting in his lap and they were both watching the spelling bee, even though neither one of them could spell.

We were eleven now. We were all out of magic powers but we would be best friends forever and that was good enough for me. Atticus looked at me and smiled. I smiled back.

Then we went back to watching the bee.

ACKNOWLEDGMENTS

This is my first book and I have many wonderful people to thank for their unwavering guidance and support:

To Susan Hawk, my superstar agent at The Bent Agency. You believed in me and Avalon when we weren't quite ready for the world yet. You absolutely changed my life and I will be forever grateful. Huge thanks to you and Jenny Bent.

To Anna Roberto, my insightful editor at Feiwel and Friends, for adopting me and making me feel so at home. To Lauren Burniac, for championing the book in the first place. And to Jean Feiwel and the awesome team at Macmillan, including Starr Baer, Liz Dresner, Veronica Ambrose, and Risa Rodil.

To my first enthusiastic young readers: Karyn Davis, Will Edwards, Kate Hirshberg, Jack Healey, and Ruby Wenzlaff.

To Ronna Anderson's fourth-grade class at Lumpkin County Elementary School, Dahlonega, Georgia; to Julie Zeldin's fifth-grade class at Odyssey Charter School, Altadena, California; and to Gemma Hawksworth's Year Three Class at St Luke's Halsall Church of England Primary School, Crosby, England— it was so much fun to share early drafts with you. And to Caroline Rairigh, who proved to me once and for all that Avalon was indeed a fifth grader!

To my cool nieces, nephews, and assorted god-kids who activate my playful heart and make me so proud: Gemma, Karyn, Will, Kathryn, Sam, Sierra, Aubrey, Luke, Jake, Matty, and Duncan. I love you guys.

To Heather Place, Joy Brown, Margaret Anne Smith, and Lori Bertazzon for your support and friendship every step of the way. And to Kate McLaughlin, my rockstar writing partner and dear friend.

To Graham Edwards for always reading fast and encouraging me to keep going, and to Kevin Gregg for coaching me when I really needed it most!

Special thanks to my extremely supportive family: my aunts, uncles, and cousins; my grandmother, Helen Paris; my sisters, Lisa Davis and Sally Edwards; and my parents, Guy and Anita Middleton, to whom this book is dedicated.

Lastly, to my first and favorite reader, my husband, Pete. Twenty feet to the sky, moonpal.

THANK YOU FOR READING THIS
FEIWEL AND FRIENDS BOOK.

The Friends who made

THE **INFINITY** years OF AVALON James

possible are:

JEAN FEIWEL, Publisher

LIZ SZABLA, Editor in Chief

RICH DEAS, Senior Creative Director

HOLLY WEST, Editor

DAVE BARRETT, Executive Managing Editor

RAYMOND ERNESTO COLÓN, Senior Production Manager

ANNA ROBERTO, Editor

CHRISTINE BARCELLONA, Associate Editor

EMILY SETTLE, Administrative Assistant

ANNA POON, Editorial Assistant

Follow us on Facebook or visit us online at mackids.com.

OUR BOOKS ARE FRIENDS FOR LIFE